Secrets on

Tobacco Road

DANIELLE SILER

SECRETS ON TOBACCO ROAD

Secrets on Tobacco Road

Published in the United States

of America ISBN 13:

9780615660684

ISBN 10: 0615660681

1. Fiction / African American / Historical
2. History / United States / Civil War Period

DANIELLE SILER

Secrets on

Tobacco Road

2nd Edition

Danielle Siler

DANIELLE SILER

Book Dedication

This book is dedicated to my two beautiful daughters, Jasmine and Jaylen, who give me the motivation to continue reaching for the stars. To wonderful husband and best friend Chad, I love you more than words can say. To my bonus daughters Zylah and Zahria, DNA could never determine and circumstance can never change your places in my heart. Last but by far not least, to my wonderful Graves & Siler families for always standing behind me, supporting me and catching me when I fall; without you, I would not have made it this far. I love you all!

Acknowledgment

I would like to acknowledge my agent, attorney and friend Nicole Moore for believing in me and my talent; and never letting me give up on my dreams! Thank You!

SECRETS ON TOBACCO ROAD

Prologue

The Devereux plantation on Tobacco Road is haunted by a lifetime of forbidden affairs; devious plots; and secret blood ties that will bind three families in misery, deception and murder for generations to come.

The story begins in New Orleans in the 1800s before the Civil War. The patriarchs of two affluent families, Peter Devereux and Alexander Marchand, devised a plan to link their families and their fortunes to become a powerful force in New Orleans. But a forbidden love affair between the sole heir of the Devereux fortune, John, and a beautiful slave girl Marie, could destroy them all.

John Devereux, Helena Marchand and Marie Jean-Batiste's friendship surpassed class and color. John and Helena were both from wealthy families and Marie and her family were slaves on the Devereux plantation.

Growing up Helena had always had a crush on John, but his heart had secretly belonged to Marie; a fact that would prove to be of deadly consequence to them both. As
time progresses, so does the feelings that began to develop between John and Marie; and so, does the jealously and obsession that was growing in Helena.

When John reached the age of 21 and Helena 20, their families arranged for them to be married; merging their families' assets and social status. Peter Devereux stressed to both his son and his new daughter in law that it was of the utmost importance that a child be born of their union to complete their families' fusion. But because of an infection that was left untreated, Helena was unable to carry a child; making it impossible for her to conceive the heir both families had hoped for.

This news was more than a devastating blow to Helena whose childhood crush on John had grown to a deadly fixation. To add to Helena's anguish, it was soon revealed that Marie and John had given in to their growing love for one another and shared a forbidden night of passion.

The act of betrayal alone was enough to send Helena over the edge; but as a result of that night Marie was able to give John something Helena could not, not just one, but two heirs to the Devereux family name and fortune.

Marie gave birth to twin boys; one bearing the darker complexion of his mother and the other the fair skin of his father. Noticing the disparity between his two grandchildren, Peter Devereux hatched a sinister plot. Marie had unwittingly given him the answer to his prayers; and the beginning of her nightmares.

With a little creative reasoning, Peter proposed that the fairer child be raised as the son of John and Helena, while the darker sibling is raised by Marie as a slave. To make the story more convincing, Marie was forced to marry a slave named Thomas

Childress and raise her remaining son as his. Being a slave gave Marie no rights and therefore no power to refuse Peter Devereux's insidious proposal.

Although Peter's arrangement had resolved the issue of producing an heir through selective paternity, he could not resolve New Orleans society's knowledge of his deeds. He could not take the chance that after all his hard work to get his family to the status he craved; someone could reveal his deception and bring his world crashing down around him. It would be impossible for Peter's plan to work with everyone knowing so many intimate details of the Devereux's life; so, when a distant uncle in North Carolina passed away willing Peter his tobacco plantation, he moved his family and all their secrets to Tobacco Road. Unfortunately for Peter Devereux, secrets never stay buried for long.

DANIELLE SILER

SECRETS ON TOBACCO ROAD

Child's Play

Spring 1841

"Ready or not here I come!" John shouted from behind covered eyes. John and his two childhood friends, Marie and Helena were playing hide and go seek against the rich backdrop of the Louisiana Bayou. On a balmy spring day with the flowers blooming, three little children darted around magnolia trees laughing without a care in the world. You would hardly guess that in a place so beautiful, there was an ugliness that permeated its very fiber.

At the tender age of six, it was not fully understood that your skin color determines your social status, but this lesson does not go unlearned for long. John and Helena, heirs to two of the wealthiest families in New Orleans made no distinction between themselves and Marie, the heir to a life of slavery on the Devereux plantation; at least not at first.

I got you!" John screamed as he caught Helena coming from her hiding place near the front porch.

"No fair you were peeking!" Helena laughed, with her massive mound of fiery red curls now a bit disheveled atop her head. Although she had the appearance and demeanor of a proper little southern lady, her attitude was as fiery as her hair; and her emerald green eyes complimented by her milky white skin, gave her a distinctive look. While John was reveling in his victory of catching Helena, Marie darted right past him and made it safely to home base.

Standing there in her homemade dress and worn shoes, Marie stood as proud as if she was donning a wardrobe fit for a princess; and her regal looks surpassed her clothing and her station. Tall with slender build, Marie could easily be a tomboy; but her adorable face with light caramel colored skin framed by long coal black hair, let you know there was still a little girl hiding in there.

"Dang! I can't never catch you Marie!" John said in his adorable southern drawl.

"And you ain't never gonna, 'cause I'm the fastest!" Marie squealed with triumph while jumping around.

John couldn't help laughing and flashing his endearing smile as he watched Marie jump around. Even at his young age, you could tell he was going to grow into a handsome man. His curly sandy blond hair framed an adorable boyish face that was complete with the cutest set of dimples. Although he was average in height and stature for a boy his age, his presence was already larger than life; and he was already catching the attention of Louisiana's little southern belles, as well as those not born into privilege.

The three children laughed as they lay down on the fresh grass and stared up at the sky. "We are gonna be bestest friends forever and, ever right?" John said.

"Right!" the two girls exclaimed.

"Pinky swears?" John asked as he held up his pinky.

"Pinky swear" the girls shouted as they linked their pinkies with his.

Laying there laughing and enjoying the breeze, none of the children knew that after that day, their lives and their relationship would never be the same.

The children decided to go into the main house and get a glass of the ice-cold lemonade Marie's mother Sarah was making in the kitchen. Marie's family, the Jean-Baptistes, was rumored to be somehow related to Jean Baptiste Le Moyne, the Governor of the French colony of Louisiana who founded the city of New Orleans in 1718. But their more direct lineage was through that of Marie Laveau, the infamous voodoo queen of New Orleans; Marie was named for her.

Marie's family was what those in New Orleans called Creole; and they were considered one of the luckier slave families. Their lighter complexion made them house slaves, which meant that they didn't work in the field and they didn't live in the slave quarters.

In addition, no one objected to the children playing together. In fact, the Devereuxs considered themselves to be a sophisticated and enlightened Christian family, who treated their slaves well. The fact that holding human beings as your personal property while using them as unpaid servants and sources of sadistic sexual pleasures, was at best immoral and reprehensible, never entered their minds.

Sarah was a small framed woman whose chiseled features and bone structure indicated that she was once a very beautiful woman. Years of life as a slave had taken a toll on her body and spirit, but her beauty still showed through. Like Marie, Sarah's skin was a beautiful light caramel color and her long coal black hair was often pulled back smoothly into a perfect bun.

The children finished their lemonade and decided to continue their game of hide and seek in the house. The noise of squealing children caught the attention of John's father Peter Devereux, who was trying to enjoy reading his newspaper. "What the hell is going on out here?" Peter shouted as he came upon the children playing in the house. "Get on out in the yard with all that racket; I'm trying to read the paper!"

Although he was a man of average height and build, Peter Devereux was quite the ladies' man. His average looks were heightened by his impeccable taste in clothing which made him appealing to the eye. And once a lady was close enough to be wooed by his southern charm, she was like putty in his hands.

Quite charismatic, people loved to be in Peter's presence; add in his considerable fortune and social status and you had the makings of every woman's dream. However equal to his charm was his reputation for being a man whom very few were brave enough to cross. Calm and calculating with an appetite for vengeance, he was known to be relentless when it was something that he wanted or someone he wanted to destroy.

Not wanting to incite Peter to cut their fun short, the children scurried out into the yard to continue their game until it was time for John to come in for supper; and it was time for Helena to return to her home at the neighboring plantation. It never bothered Marie that her family had to eat in the kitchen or that their rooms were not as nice as the Devereuxs'. To her, they were the Devereuxs' employees and that was the only distinction. This illusion would cause Marie much heartache and unhappiness in the very near future.

Later that day, Peter's uncle Thaddeus came for a visit from North Carolina, where he owned a successful tobacco plantation. Although Uncle Thaddeus shared the same last name as Peter, he held very different ideals; especially about how slaves should interact with their masters. Thaddeus was a proud man who always walked with his shoulders back and chest puffed out as if he owned the world. Now old age had made him rely on support from a walking cane to get around.

Although an inch or two taller than Peter, their familial connection was apparent. Thaddeus was quite the handsome fellow in his day, but his devilish good looks had long vanished and all was left was the devil. His pure gray hair, cold steel blue eyes clouded by cataracts and withered face made him appear as repulsive outside as he was inside.

Upon his arrival at his nephew's plantation, he spied the children playing their usual game of hide-and-seek in the yard. Thinking it quite unacceptable that a slave child, no matter how light, should fancy herself good enough to play with white children; Uncle Thaddeus felt it was his duty as a good white Christian to set his nephew straight on the natural order of things.

With fire in his eyes Thaddeus stepped out of his carriage and right into Marie, who was engrossed in running from her usual playmates John and Helena. Although she neither bumped into Thaddeus intentionally nor hard enough to hurt him, her mistake drew harsh consequences. Smack! Thaddeus smacked Marie across the face with his cane and she instantly fell to the ground crying incessantly and shielding her face from any additional blows.

Seeing his friend on the ground in pain and not yet fully understanding how their world operated, John ran right up and kicked Thaddeus in the leg while Helena rushed to the aid of the wounded Marie.

"You stay away from my friend or you'll need more than one cane to walk around!" John shouted with little fists balled up and standing in a fighting stance to emphasize that he meant business.

Holding his leg in pain and anger, Thaddeus raised his cane to swat down his next victim; but as he was about to induce the same fate on John as he had Marie, Peter grabbed his uncle's arm in midair

"What the hell is going on out here? Mister, I'm not sure who you are, but you better have a damn good reason for being on my property. Now I am going to give you 5 seconds to make your business known, before I introduce you to a fate far worse than a kick in the leg!" Peter shouted.

Regaining his composure, Thaddeus replied "Well I see I am just in time, things seem to be going to hell in a hand basket around here. My name's Thaddeus Devereux; and I'm your late father's oldest brother."

Standing in disbelief, Peter released his uncle's arm and said "Uncle Thaddeus? I thought you were dead."

Straightening his now rumpled clothing, Thaddeus replied, "Well as you can see I am neither spirit nor specter so surely I am not dead. Now kindly invite me in and I'll state my purpose for being here."

Peter paused briefly, then slowly stepped aside and motioned for Thaddeus to go in the house. And Sarah who heard the commotion, ran to the aid of her child, scooping her up in her arms and checking her injuries.

Once inside, Thaddeus revealed his purpose for being there. "I realize that we have never laid eyes on one another, but that was because I was what some may call the 'black sheep' of the family. I lived my life according to my rules and my rules alone, but that didn't quite sit right with my father. So, at the age of eighteen, I set out on my own and never looked back. James, my baby brother and your father, was my parent's only other child; and once I left, my father vowed that I was dead to him and that my name should be erased from memory."

He said pouring himself a drink and taking a sip before continuing his story.

"This was well before you were born and although I never went back home, I still kept up with everything that was going on with the family. When your father died, I knew the only person I gave a damn about was gone forever and I had no reason to ever return."

With a steady gaze Peter quizzed "So why are you here now? You didn't come back for my father, so what business do you want with me?"

Breaking from his solemn trip down memory lane, Thaddeus replied "You and your family are my only living relatives and I am an old man; I'd like to get to know you while I'm still on this earth".

Peter felt that his unexpected visit from his uncle was about more than he was saying, but he indulged the old man anyway.

Looking around at his nephew's house, Thaddeus stated "You have a fine plantation here son, now you need to treat it as such."

Looking visibly insulted Peter responded, "Excuse me?"

Never being one to mince words, Thaddeus immediately gave his nephew his unsolicited opinion on how he should run things. "This is a plantation son, and plantations are powered by slaves! Slaves; not respected employees or playmates for your children like they are here! Slaves aren't people son; they're on the same level as your cattle or your mules. They're property the good lord sent to us white folks for being his chosen people. Like a gift; a gift that we can use any way we please. The good Lord knew we needed to eat and that to do that we needed to be able to plow the fields and pick the crops, but he didn't want us to have to do that. No sir, we are made in his own image; that's why we have our lily-white skin. It's too delicate to be out in that heat all day." Thaddeus said, pausing for effect.

"We weren't made for manual labor son. But God made the niggers so that they could do all the things for us that we are too good to do ourselves. Why do you think they got that dark skin? So, they can stand being in the sun. Why do you think they are strong as an ox? So, they can carry heavy loads just as any other animal. Now you mark my words son, the only way to keep those darkies in line is to instill fear in them; otherwise they're going to go thinking they're one of us and expect to be treated as such. Then you are gonna have mutiny on your hands!" Thaddeus exclaimed, and then took another sip of his drink before continuing his sermon.

"Take a lesson from your old Uncle Thaddeus. When one of those darkies steps out of line hang'em high for all to see; or if he is a strong buck and you need to keep'em around to work the fields, then just beat him within an inch of his life and rub salt in the wounds so they'll have a painful reminder of how things go. Then he'll think twice about trying to live above his station!" Thaddeus said with a laugh.

"Just like that little nigger gal that ran into me outside, I bet she'll learn to mind her step in the company of white folks. And your boy, coming to the rescue of a slave; what are you teaching him? You best tell him if he behaves like a slave he'll be punished like a slave!" Uncle Thaddeus ended his tirade by poking his nephew in the chest to emphasize his last statement.

Having heard enough of Uncle Thaddeus' rant and not appreciating his taking liberty by poking him, Peter first looked down at his uncle's boney finger in his chest, the slowly raised his eyes to meet his uncle's gaze.

"Make that the last time you touch me." Peter instructed with a slow deliberate tone, while removing his uncle's finger.

"Now you listen good old man, 'cause I'll not say it again, how I run my house or deal with my slaves and my son is my business; and the next time you get the urge to discipline either, the time you have left on this earth will get a whole lot shorter." He said before breaking his stare.

"Out of respect for my father's memory you are welcome to stay the night, but in the morning, you best be making your way back to North Carolina. Dinner is promptly at 6 o'clock; Thomas will take your things to your room. And Uncle Thaddeus, I trust that you will mind your manners and keep your cane on the ground where it belongs for the remainder of your stay in my house." Peter stated before exiting and instructing Thomas, a light complexioned slave boy, to take Uncle Thaddeus' things to one of the guest rooms.

Staring in silence as he watched his nephew exit the room, Thaddeus followed Thomas to his sleeping quarters without another word. He didn't agree with his ideals, but he admired his nephew's determination to be his own man and live by his own rules; a trait Thaddeus recognized and lived by. Meanwhile, Sarah nursed her daughter's wounds while teaching her a lesson she wished she never had to learn.

"Momma, why did that man hit me?" Marie asked through teary eyes and swollen lips.

Trying to fight back the tears in her own eyes, Sarah responded gently "because you a slave baby and white folks can do whatever they want to you. I know you don't understand now and I would give my life if you never had to, but its best you know now, so you can know what type of life is waiting for you out there." Sarah continued to place ice on her daughter's face while she taught her about what it meant to be a slave.

"Now Master Devereux is one of the better White folks as far as Masters go, but don't you think for one minute that means that he cares nothing 'bout any of us. To him and every other White person we are just property, just like them cows in that field out there. Mister Thaddeus, he is like most of the White folks you gonna meet in this world baby, mean as a copperhead snake and twice as deadly." Sarah warned.

"They got no soul; can't have a soul and cause the type of pain and suffering White folks have caused colored folks all they life. You be careful baby and mind what I say. If you see a White person coming, stay away from them for your own safety; and if they say something to you, just say yes sir or yes ma'am and be on your way." Sarah said looking into her daughter's sorrowful eyes.

"White folks will make you feel dirty, like you ain't nothing but the slop they feed the pigs with, but that's not true. You are beautiful baby and no matter what White folks do to you, remember that. They can take your life, but they can't take your pride. Just be careful and be smart. This world can't stay like this forever. The good Lord wouldn't be that cruel. Change is gonna come, we just have to hold on 'til it gets here; and until it does, you have to live by the rules I just gave you, 'cause there are some White folks out here that will kill you just because they can. Remember that baby; and while Mister Thaddeus is here, you stay clear of him." Sarah instructed.

With eyes full of tears and lips trembling, Marie replied "Yes Ma'am".

Marie went back outside, but she didn't feel like playing anymore. Since her run in with Thaddeus' cane and the talk with her mother, Marie's world and her best friends looked very different to her now. Seeing their friend emerge from the house, John and Helena rushed to her side to comfort her.

"I don't care who he is, he ain't no uncle of mine; and I'll kick him in his other leg if he tries to hurt you again Marie." John said in a matter of fact tone.

"Yeah," Helena agreed.

Marie joined her friends on the porch swing, but she didn't forget the lesson her mother had just taught her. She sat in silence for the rest of the day. But unbeknownst to Thaddeus, Sarah had passed by the study on her way to the kitchen to get ice for her daughter's face; and she heard Thaddeus' little lesson he was giving Peter on how to maim and even kill slaves to keep them in their place. Sarah decided then and there that her daughter was not the only person she intended to teach a lesson.

Being a descendent of a voodoo queen meant that Sarah knew more than enough to avenge her daughter; and being a house slave gave her all the access she needed to Thaddeus' personal belongings to make whatever gris-gris she wanted. She would make sure her daughter and the slaves unfortunate enough to be under Thaddeus would not be the only ones feeling pain.

Sarah went to Thaddeus' room to gather some personal belongings. While looking for something she could use to cast a spell, she bumped into the dresser and a small brown journal fell to the floor. She picked it up thinking it would contain something she could use against Thaddeus, but as she read, it became clear that the journal didn't belong to him; it belonged to Peter's wife Elizabeth Devereux.

Sarah only read the first page, but its contents were so jarring that she dropped the journal. Snapping back to reality, Sarah continued with her mission of why she was there, but the memory of what she had read was seared in her mind. She put the journal back but was in such a hurry that she didn't realize that it was still visible.

Returning to her original purpose, Sarah found a comb on the dresser with some of Thaddeus' hair still in it. She took the hair and placed it in a small cloth bag and returned to the kitchen to prepare dinner. Sarah made a special dish for Thaddeus, seasoned with herbs that had been prepared to carry out the spell she intended to cast on him.

Later that night, with the gris-gris around her neck containing Thaddeus' hair, Sarah served her special dish to the unexpected guest of honor. Unaware of how he was about to pay for his prior offense towards Marie, Thaddeus consumed the deadly meal.

When dinner was over, and everyone had retired to bed, Sarah sat up in her room chanting while twisting the gris-gris in her hand. Lying in his bed, Thaddeus began to feel sick. It was as if someone was twisting his stomach in knots. The pain was so great that he could not even cry out. At one point he even thought he was going to die, but Sarah had no intention of killing Thaddeus. However, she did intend to ensure that by the time she was through with him, he would wish for death as he would a lover's kiss.

The next day, having recovered from his night of pain, Thaddeus packed his belongings to go home. His trip did not go exactly as he had planned, but he was happy he was able to see his nephew. *Maybe if I had been around more when he was growing up, he wouldn't be so naïve to how the world really works* Thaddeus considered.

He has a strong mind and he is as stubborn as an ox. With the right direction and coaxing he could have been a slave master and businessman to rival all others, but alas I fear I am too late to bear any influence on him at this point. It would seem my very presence plagues him with irritation, but he is the only family I have left, he deliberated as he continued to gather his things.

Thaddeus was so engrossed in reflection that he dropped his cufflink on the floor. When he bent to pick it up; he saw an old brown journal sticking out. His curiosity was peaked; and he picked it up and began to read. The pages had started to turn yellow from age, but the secrets it contained were still remarkably clear. The words that were written on the first page alone made Thaddeus' blood run cold; and he quickly packed the journal in with his belongings.

Gathering the remainder of his things, he called for Thomas to come and take them to the carriage. His long trip back to North Carolina would afford him ample opportunity to finish reading the rest of the journal; and try to forget the last 24 hours that he spent writhing in pain. He thought maybe his sudden illness was due to something that he ate; and that the worse of it was behind him, but he couldn't have been more wrong. Although Thaddeus had been released from his recent brush with death; his nightmare was far from over. Sarah held on to the Gris- Gris she made for him, because she was by no means done making Thaddeus suffer.

Southern Comfort

Winter 1855

When Thaddeus returned to North Carolina, he went to every specialist he could find to seek relief from his mysterious illness; but no doctor could diagnose his ailment. From that faithful day he visited his nephew in New Orleans and every day for years to come, he suffered terrible stomach pains that kept him up at night praying   for God to relieve his suffering or be kind enough to bring death to end it.

The years crept by and Thaddeus continued to get weaker and weaker, but no end to his suffering was in sight. Just as Sarah predicted, Thaddeus wished for death, but death would not come for him for several more years.

Back in New Orleans, the passage of time had caused some very different changes. Peter Devereux was a man of average stature and good looks. His short dark brown hair and dark brown eyes were nothing particularly unique, but his charm and charismatic demeanor made him simply irresistible to the women of New Orleans; coupled with the fact that he was now extremely rich and powerful made him a prime catch.

Proving that the apple doesn't fall far from the tree, his son John was also blessed with Peter's southern charms; but as an added bonus he also inherited his mother's stunning good looks and her kind heart. John Devereux had grown into his curly sandy blonde hair and a boyish smile complete with dimples. He was average height like his father, but his chiseled physique was anything but average. Young women all over Louisiana would swoon at the sight of that dimpled smile and get lost in those beautiful blue eyes. They would hang on every word that exited his mouth wrapped in his adorable southern drawl.

Marie had grown into a vision of beauty; a beauty that surpassed her station in life. She was tall with light caramel complexioned skin that was remarkably smooth. Her slim, yet feminine physique was accented by her stunningly beautiful face; and her kind spirit was evidenced in the striking smile that she wore as effortlessly as she breathed. Her mother Sarah shared her caramel complexion and slim build, but she was of shorter stature. Although still a very attractive woman, the years of living life as a slave were as visible on her face as her smoldering dark eyes.

By contrast, Helena Marchand had become the definition of the phrase 'beauty is only skin deep, but ugly is to the bone'. She had milky white skin that draped her tall curvaceous body; and a mane of long red hair that matched her fiery personality. Spoiled and shallow, her parents bent to her every whim. Being the heir to a substantial fortune had only compounded her sense of entitlement and her arrogance, which nurtured her growing cruelty and disregard for others.

Time had not only affected physical appearances, but relationships as well; particularly in the friendship of John, Helena and Marie. As they grew into adolescents so did the attraction Helena had for John. Unfortunately for her, that protective instinct John had for Marie as a child had grown into a lover's bond that was stronger than any of them could have predicted.

Although it was forbidden and unthinkable for the two of them to be together, their attraction and love for one another was undeniable. Marie had grown to love John more than she ever thought she could love anyone outside of her family; but neither of them dared act on those feelings. That was until John and Helena's parents came up with a plan that would impact all their lives; and unwittingly link their three families together forever.

Every New Year's Eve, the Devereuxs throw one of the grandest masquerade balls New Orleans has ever seen; and everyone including the house slaves were allowed to dress up and join the fun. The field slaves were allowed to take over the duties normally carried out by the house slaves.

Although they were still working, they were allowed to dress up; and the chores of carrying a tray around seemed like a Christmas present compared to carrying heavy bales of cotton. In the mind of the Devereuxs, this once a year act of generously allowing their slaves to live above their normal station somehow made them better than "other" slave masters; and therefore, God would bless them to be more prosperous for their good Christian deed. Moreover, they thought that their slaves would be less likely to revolt and murder them in their sleep.

On this particular New Year's Eve, the patriarchs of the Devereux and Marchand families met secretly before the festivities to finalize a plan they had been discussing since their children were born. They would arrange for their children John and Helena to wed, merging their families and their fortunes to become the most powerful force in New Orleans. With their combined money and influence, they could amass fortunes unmeasured by anyone else. To make this deal work, an heir must be sired from their children's union.

Once Peter Devereux and Alexander Marchand agreed that it was time to bring their long-discussed plan into fruition, they thought what better time to announce their children's engagement than that very night. New Year's Eve represented a promise of new beginnings and that is what they hoped their children's union would produce.

Each father agreed that they would speak to their children individually to inform them of their impending nuptials and prepare them for the big announcement. When they were set on how the plan would be carried out, they each left to get dressed for the party and find their respective offspring to share the big news.

There was an air of excitement at the Devereux plantation that night as everyone, including the slaves, took extra care in getting dressed for the evening's festivities. In Marie's small corner bedroom, she prepared herself for the one night of the year when she could pretend that she was not a slave. Instead, she imagined that she was preparing to attend only one of many balls that she would be invited to that year. Marie bathed in a bath of milk and honey; and dusted herself with powder, to ensure that her smooth skin would remain dry during all of the dancing she intended to do that evening.

Marie carefully pulled on her hose and knee length linen chemise; because she was naturally shapely, she did not need to wear a corset as most women in high society did when attending formal events. Once her undergarments were in place, she stepped into the beautiful satin emerald green gown her mother was allowed to make for her.

Standing there with her beautiful long dark hair in massive curls pinned atop her head, Marie looked at herself in her gown. She eyed the wide neckline, rounded bust, sloping shoulders, short puffed elbow length sleeves accentuated by white satin gloves, and the narrow waist and full hips which she filled out naturally.

Staring at her reflection, she felt like a princess in a fairytale and the only prince she wanted to kiss was John. Thinking of being able to steal a dance and moment with him made her heart flutter. At least for tonight, their worlds could merge without threat or shame; tonight, she could dance in the arms of her true love.

In the opposite wing of the estate, John was also thinking of his true love Marie. As he dressed in his balloon sleeved shirt and perfectly tailored coat and trousers, he let himself drift off into a daydream. He was dressing for his wedding day and he was to marry Marie. In his daydream there were no restrictions, no slaves and masters; people were free to love who they loved. This was unusual thinking for his time and thoughts that could surely cause a stir if stated aloud. Not wanting to waste one minute of his time he could spend with Marie, John prepared to go search for her; but before he could leave, his father came into the room.

"There is my handsome son," Peter stated, intercepting John at the door.

"Hello Father; I was just headed downstairs to greet the guests." John lied, hoping his father would not further keep him from his quest.

"Spare a minute for your old Father; I have some big news to share with you." Peter said ushering his son back in the room.

"What kind of news?" John asked anxious to be done with whatever conversation his father had in mind."

Peter offered his son one of the drinks he had brought to smooth over his news of an arranged marriage, and then broke the news.

"Son, ever since your brother died I have tried to prepare you to take over the family business. I have tried to teach you about seeing the big picture and the potential of certain…mergers in life. Well now that you're twenty-one, it's time that you make an important step in that direction. Every powerful man in polite society has a wife by his side. Those who are blessed with the good sense God gave them will make that choice based on benefit more so than love. Love is fleeting son, but power is forever." Peter declared.

Looking confused and very apprehensive about what his father was proposing; John tried to swallow the lump that was now forming in his throat, as a sudden sense of dread filled his body. Ignoring the fact that his son suddenly looked as if he was about to be sentenced to death, Peter continued.

"John, I know you have been sniffing around Marie for some time now; and don't get me wrong, the wiles of the slave women far exceed those of the white ones, so I understand your attraction. But as pretty as she is, Marie is and always will be a slave; which means she can never be anything more than a concubine used to exercise your carnal pleasures with. Trust me son, I know who and what is best for you; and that's why tonight, you'll be announcing your engagement to Helena Marchand, "Peter said as nonchalantly as he would order his morning coffee.

John felt as though the wind had been knocked out of his body as he tried to wrap his mind around what his father had just said. Finally, he managed to stammer out "Helena? She is nothing more than a friend to me father; a childhood playmate."

Taking a sip of his whisky, Peter replied, "Yes, but she is not a child anymore, now is she? No, she is a full-grown woman who has obvious feelings for you. Use that to your advantage son. The Marchand

Empire is the only one in New Orleans that rivals our own. Having a wife from a wealthy and influential family to do your bidding is priceless. And the beauty is that you don't have to worry about your judgment being clouded by loving her back."

Peter spun the proposition of making Helena John's wife like a storyteller would a fairytale. But John knew there would be no happy ending for him or Marie. Resigning to his fate, John agreed to marry Helena as his father wished; and in return, his father offered him one night with Marie. Knowing that was the best he could glean from this duplicitous deal, John set off to find Marie.

Meanwhile Alexander Marchand had no problems convincing his daughter to marry John. Over the years Helena's feelings for John had grown from friendship, to love, to deadly obsession. Once she learned that she was to be engaged to John at the Masquerade Ball, Helena took extra care with getting ready.

Through sinister grin she hummed the wedding march as she sprayed her skin with expensive Lavender water and fluffed the curls in her hair. She happily grabbed her mask for the ball and took her father's arm as he escorted her to her dream destiny.

At the Devereux Plantation, the party was just beginning, and the house was filled with New Orleans' high society. John feigned a smile as he spoke to the arriving guests, then put on his mask and continued his quest to find Marie. She was just entering the ballroom when John grabbed her by the hand and took her up the back stairs to his room.

With an excited giggle, Marie followed John to his room. She looked so beautiful in her gown; and her smile was only rivaled by the sparkle of happiness and excitement in her eyes. How could he tell her he was to marry Helena? How could he hurt her like that? He had protected her since they were children, but now there was no one that could protect her from the pain he himself was about to cause.

Before John could bring himself to ruin what was supposed to be their one perfect night, he just wanted to   hold her in his arms and kiss her tenderly. He wanted to hold on to a perfect moment and image of her before he was forced into his marriage of convenience.

After breaking from their passionate embrace, John led Marie over to the bed to sit down. With solemn eyes, he stated, "Marie, you are so beautiful, and I will love you until there is no more breath in my body nor beat in my heart; that's why it pains me to have to say this to you…" And just like the changing of the wind, the smile began to disappear from Marie's face as she felt her heart pounding in her chest.

John looked away for a moment to regain his composure. Then he continued, "Marie, my father has struck a deal that I must carry out."

Now feeling her body start to go numb, Marie asked "What kind of deal?"

John filled her in on his father's plan for his arranged marriage to Helena and Marie felt as if someone had snatched her soul right out of her body. Tears filled her eyes and flowed freely down her face. Fighting back tears of his own, John begged that she forgive him and that they have one night together, so that he may show her that she is the one that he will forever love.

As John and Marie fell into each other's arms, they made love for the first time. It was the most beautiful experience either had ever known, but it was tinged with pain and sadness. No matter how much they loved each other, society's rules prevented them from being together. As he kissed Marie slowly and tenderly, John whispered "My father may order that my body be delivered to Helena, but until its final beat, my heart will forever be yours."

The two lovers were so engrossed in each other that neither heard the door creep open. Nor did they notice that Helena was standing there to hear John's proclamation of love to a slave over the one that is to be his wife. Enraged, Helena ran down the stairs in search of someone to help   her exact revenge. She bumped into the cousin of one of her childhood friends. He was visiting from Atlanta and asked if Helena would like to dance. She declined his offer to dance but countered with another that he could not refuse. In the heat of anger, Helena gave her body to a man that was not her intended, and her careless actions would   cost her dearly.

While the party was in full swing, both John and Helena were giving their bodies to someone else. Helena gave hers to a random conquest to soothe her bruised ego; and John gave his to his true love to soothe his broken heart. When their perfect moment was over, John said goodbye to Marie, then went to face his destiny with Helena.

By the time he arrived in the ballroom, Helena had finished her meaningless romp and was coming in as well. She stood there with hell burning in her eyes, but through a sweet smile asked "Why John where have you been sweetheart, I have been looking all over the place for you. What on earth could have kept you from a party in our honor?" John looked her in the eyes, but gave no response as he walked to stand by his father for the announcement.

"Ladies and gentlemen, may I have your attention please?" Peter asked as he chimed his glass with his fork. "It is my great pleasure to announce to you all, the engagement of my son John to Miss Helena Marchand!"

The crowd erupted in claps and well wishes; and Helena ate up every minute of it. John, on the other hand, blocked out the remainder of the night. As he looked at his impending bride he thought his father had made a deal with the devil, brokered by Satan himself.

Marie had been quietly standing in the back of the room watching with broken heart and spirit, as the man she loved was promised to another. She had never remembered experiencing so much pain before, she felt as if her heart was being ripped out of her chest.

Helena smiled at all the well-wishers that moved through a procession like line to offer their individual congratulations to the couple. When Marie made her way to the unhappy couple, she looked at the floor as she forced out the words

"Congratulations; I am happy for you both".

With a razor-sharp stare Helena replied "Well Marie darling, I am almost inclined to think you don't mean that; you almost seemed to choke on the words. Is something wrong old friend?"

Not wanting to subject Marie to any more torture than she was already having to endure, he interjected "Leave her alone, Helena." Then he turned to Marie and said, "Thank you Marie. Your mother was looking for you earlier; I think she said she was going to your room to search for you."

John offered Marie an escape from Helena's piercing gaze and she gladly took it. After murmuring a soft 'thank you' to John, Marie hurried off to her room where she could nurse her broken heart in private.

Although she had succeeded in making Marie upset, Helena's victory was a hollow one. Even now, at a celebration that was to signify their new life together, John was protecting her. Feeling that John had once again put Marie's feelings above her own, the fire in Helena's eyes was once again ignited and she directed her rage to John. She turned to him with a sarcastic smile and said "Careful sweetheart; you wouldn't want to give the impression that you value a slave over your wife. What do you think people would think of you then…what kind of man treats a dog better than the love of his life?"

Not amused by Helena's words, John gripped her arm and pulled her so close their noses were almost touching; and through a feign smile marred by clinched teeth and rage he spat. "You're the one who should be careful sweetheart; this isn't the back yard and I am beyond the days of childhood games. Now let's get something straight, my father may be forcing me into this farce of a marriage with you, but you are not by any stretch of the imagination, the love of my life. So, you see darling I am following proper protocol...Marie is the love of my life, and I am not the type of man that would place a bitch above her."

A stunned Helena stood there visibly shaking as John released her arm and nonchalantly walked away to mingle with the other guests. Helena's hatred for Marie reached dangerous proportions; and fueled the jealousy she secretly harbored for her since they were children. Her impromptu tryst with her friend's cousin didn't vindicate the crime Marie had committed by stealing John's heart; no for that crime, she had only begun to make Marie pay.

Chapter Three

Unholy Matrimony

Spring 1856

Over the next several months, Helena threw herself into making plans for the biggest wedding New Orleans had ever seen. She tabled her hatred for Marie and the knowledge of John's hatred for her; long enough to delude herself into thinking this was a real wedding. Her father had the best seamstress in New Orleans making her a one   of a kind wedding dress from Japanese hand spun silk; and French lace shipped from the most expensive garment house in Paris.

Helena and her mother Olivia went through all the proper ceremonial processes that any normal bride in love would do. The only problem was that Helena was neither a normal bride or in love...she was her father's willing bargaining chip and she was obsessed with John.   Olivia played into the fantasy that her daughter was about to embark on her dream journey captained by the wedding of a lifetime. She arranged for the June wedding ceremony to be held at St. Louis Cathedral, the oldest and biggest church in New Orleans; and planned her daughter's bridal tea to be held at their family home.

Preparation leading up to this and every other wedding event was handled with great care and detail. The events were so grand and planned in such a short time period, that the house slaves from both the Marchand and the Devereux plantations were enlisted to help. For Helena, this not only meant that she would have more assistance pulling her dream wedding together, it also meant that she could make the process a nightmare for Marie; a thought that made her almost as excited as the wedding itself.

Three weeks before her bridal tea, Helena made Marie her personal lady in waiting. She was to be at Helena's beck and call as she readied herself to marry the only man Marie had ever loved. Each day was more torturous than the next as Helena forced Marie to endure her sadistic taunting about how she and John were going to live happily ever after. If that wasn't enough, Helena also threatened to sell her to a sadistic slave master named Winston Dubois, who had wanted Marie for years.

Winston did not come from an affluent family and he was definitely not part of New Orleans' elite, but his appetite for rape and torture were legendary. He was a large grotesque man and he paid no attention to hygiene and grooming. His rotting teeth caused a stench in his mouth comparable to the smell of a dead animal; and all of his slaves lived in quarters similar to stalls meant for animals. The thought of being sold to him, made Marie's blood run cold. At that moment Marie decided if Helena were to sell her to Winston Dubois, she would kill herself before he ever got the chance to touch her.

The weeks had seemed to roll on like years as the day of Helena's bridal tea finally arrived. Marie had been feeling nauseated for a while, but had brushed it off as being upset by the pending nuptials. Marie's mother Sarah had noticed that her daughter had not been herself lately as well. Finally, Sarah confronted Marie in the kitchen about her suspicions. Walking up and grabbing Marie's arm, Sarah quizzed, "You pregnant girl?"

As she spun Marie around to face her, Marie answered with lips trembling, "I don't know."

Instantly feeling ashamed under her mother's glare, Marie held her stomach and cast her eyes down on the floor.

"Lord Girl! Miz Helena gonna sell you for sure when she finds out you carrying her husband's baby!" Sarah said in a hushed tone. The tears instantly began to flow, and Sarah could not stand there and watch her child carry this burden alone. Taking her in a protective embrace, Sarah tried to shelter her daughter from the anguish she knew in her soul was coming.

"Don't you say nothing to nobody about this, you hear?" Sarah warned, and then said. "I'm going to take care of it.

There's an old woman who's a midwife from Africa; she can make sure that baby never comes."

Tears flowed heavier from Marie's eyes and she shouted "no momma, I don't want to kill my baby. It's the only thing I have of John that I can love!"

Covering her daughter's mouth and looking around to see if anyone was listening, Sarah said "have you lost your sense child? Miz Helena will have you killed before she let you have Master Devereux's child."

Standing with new found courage, Marie replied, "Then I will just have to die; because I am not going to kill my baby".

With pain in her eyes, she watched her child show the first signs of a mother's love, the willingness to trade her life for that of her child. A feeling Sarah knew all too well; because although she knew this was not going to end well for her daughter, she knew she would hang by the noose for slitting Helena's throat before she let her kill her child. Sarah pulled Marie in another motherly embrace as she promised not to let anyone know she was carrying John's baby.

While Sarah fully intended to keep her daughter's secret, the walls hold no such loyalty; and John overheard his lover's declaration while standing in the doorway to the kitchen. He quickly backed into the hall to process the new information. At first his heart brimmed with excitement at the thought of having a baby with Marie, but that feeling was quickly replaced with anxiety when reality brought his world crashing down. Marie was a slave and he was engaged to Helena; there was no way he could follow his heart and raise his child with Marie, but he had to figure out how to protect them.

John was aware of the threats that Helena had levied against Marie, including selling her to

Winston Dubois. There was no way he was going to let Marie and his child fall into Winston's hands, but how was he going to stop it? Anxiety quickly turned to panic as John's head began to spin with the ever-increasing thoughts that were racing through it. He needed to think of a plan, but first he needed to speak to Marie, alone.

When Sarah wasn't looking, John signaled for Marie to meet him up in his room. After signaling back that she would, she made up an excuse about having to get some things Helena had requested and left her mother to meet John. Once she arrived in his room and they were sure the coast was clear, they shared a long-awaited embrace.

Pulling her away so he could look into her eyes, John said, "I regret to say I overheard you and your mother talking in the kitchen about you carrying my child; I'm so sorry my darling. This should be a joyous occasion to be celebrated, not hidden like some dirty little secret. Unfortunately, we do not live in a time where this is possible; and my impending marriage to Helena does not help matters. I want you to know that I love you and our child; and in different times I would sweep you up in my arms and shout my joy from the rooftops. It is my greatest regret that at best I can only do my best to protect you and our unborn child from detection and harm."

This heartfelt sentiment brought tears to both lovers' eyes; but sentiment alone would not protect Marie from Helena's wrath once she knew of her pregnancy. After sharing another embrace, John and Marie parted ways. John went for a walk in the garden to clear his head and think of how he was going to protect his secret family; and Marie went to continue her tortuous task of tending to Helena's pre-nuptial needs.

Helena was talking to the florist amidst the Devereuxs' illustrious and massive garden; she wanted to include some of its signature blooms in the ceremony. However, spotting John emerging from the house looking distressed and Marie a short time later with the same look; deflected Helena's attention from floral arrangements.

As her fiancée brushed past her as if she didn't exist, Helena quickly tried to save face by calling out to him to   get his attention. Counting on John's decorum and rearing as a southern gentleman, she figured that he wouldn't dare be rude in front of strangers.

"John sweetheart, I am trying to select the best arrangements for our ceremony; something that will be a symbol of our union. Do you have any suggestions?" Helena asked, donning a nervous smile.

Stopping in his tracks, John turned around, appearing to have a genuine interest. With fictitious excitement, he said to Helena, "Why yes I do darling." Turning to the florist, John said "I would like the entire church covered in white roses and peace lilies."

Looking confused, the florist asked nervously, "These flowers best symbolize your union?"

With a sadistic smile and charming southern drawl, John replied to the florist's question while looking directly into Helena's eyes. "Definitely!

Since white roses symbolize innocence, purity and true love."

Helena smiled widely at what she thought was a beautiful sentiment; but her smile quickly faded as her intended continued with his explanation.

"See, I want the white roses there to symbolize everything that holy matrimony is supposed to be; and I want the peace lilies there to symbolize how our unholy union represents the death of all those things."

After watching the smile on Helena's face fade, John then continued on his way. Helena's embarrassment quickly turned to anger as she watched Marie approach. Since she couldn't take that anger out on John, she would most assuredly make Marie suffer the consequences.

As Marie reached Helena, she demanded that Marie immediately go pick 200 blackberries to make her favorite dessert, a blackberry cobbler. The hillside where Marie was instructed to pick these berries lay on the other side of a large wooded area. As if navigating her way through the treacherous terrain of the woods wasn't bad enough, Marie had to maneuver through unmanaged tangles of dense arching stems and branches riddled with sharp thorns to extract the sweet fruit.

Between the long journey to and from the hillside and the effort it took to not only scale the steep hill, but secure her footing while picking the fruit, Marie was exhausted. On the journey back, she began to feel faint. She was pregnant and had not eaten anything all day. The instinct to care for her baby overcame her fear of Helena's wrath and she rested by a nearby stream and ate five of the 200 berries she had just picked; and drank water she scooped from the stream with her hands.

When she emerged from the woods late that evening, she was exhausted and weak; and her hands were bloody and bruised from the blackberry's thorny stems. Marie stumbled into the house to give the berries to Helena. As she approached her with the basket of fruit, she was so delirious from hunger and exhaustion that she forgot to wipe the stain of blackberries from her lips. Detecting that Marie had sampled some of the fruit, she made her count out the berries in front of her one by one. Barely able to stand, Marie did as she was instructed and counted each berry.

When she finished with a count of 195, Helena smacked her across the face and then ordered that she be taken outside and lashed for stealing. She watched as Marie was dragged outside by an overseer, tied to a post and had her dress ripped from her body. As Marie stood there naked for all to see, Helena noticed that Marie's stomach had a slight but obvious protrusion. It did not take long for Helena to deduce that the baby was John's; or for her anger to become out of control. She ordered that Marie receive 200 lashes for the number of blackberries she was supposed to bring back.

Like a wild animal toying with her prey, Helena delighted in Marie's torture. She pulled a chair onto the porch, so she could have a front row view of her pain. With each lash, Helena squealed with delight as she ate her ill- gotten fruit and enjoyed the show. Each lash tore through the flesh on Marie's back like a knife through butter. She screamed and begged for mercy, but to no avail.

Finally, the commotion brought everyone else from the house outside, including John and Marie's mother Sarah. Seeing her daughter's blood running from her back was like a knife in Sarah's heart. Acting on impulse and instinct, John raced from the porch and threw the overseer to the ground. Enraged at what he had done, John pinned him to the ground and rained down punches on his body like a thunderstorm.

John's father Peter pulled his son off of the overseer and demanded that he control himself, but his gesture was by no means a sign that condoned his future daughter-in- law's actions. Peter's strides were so wide and hurried he reached Helena in what seemed like three steps, pulling her to her feet. His eyes burrowed into hers as he spat between clenched teeth.

"Now you listen to me little girl, you best get your emotions and jealousy under control. I don't care what happens around here that you don't like! Your last name is not Devereux as of yet; and you do not dictate anything on my property, including what happens to my slaves. Now you would do well to remember this warning, or Marie won't be the only one mixing tears and blood!"

Seeing the fire in her future father-in-law's eyes made Helena's blood run cold. She knew he was serious and she knew she would also have to face John for what she did. But the glare she didn't notice, the one that was deadlier than any of the Devereuxs, was that of Sarah. For unbeknownst to

Helena, she had just made a very deadly enemy.

Once Helena was released from Peter's grip, she quietly walked into the house without making any eye contact. She was extremely embarrassed and angry that once again Marie was treated with more concern than her. Despite this, she was careful to keep her feelings of offense to herself.

Outside, John cut Marie down, wrapped her in his jacket and carried her inside. His heart felt like it was being ripped in half; and his whole body was burning with anger. He could not bear to see Marie in pain and he felt extreme guilt; for he knew it was because of Helena's obsession with him that she hurt Marie. How can I continue to live like this? Separated from the woman I love and chained to a woman I grow to hate more and more each day? John pondered to himself as he carried Marie.

Meanwhile, Sarah went to the kitchen to get some water and rags to clean Marie's wounds and a special salve to speed her healing. As she gathered what she needed to treat her daughter, Sarah's mind was carefully calculating a treatment for Helena as well. Sarah knew that Helena had slept with another man the night of the ball; and she also knew from a slave that accompanied the man from Atlanta, that the man was infected with gonorrhea. Although, Sarah had nothing to do with Helena contracting the deadly disease, she did cast a spell to mask detection and control the damage it would do to her body.

Just as she had done with Uncle Thaddeus, Sarah made a Gris Gris from Helena's hair. She tucked it inside her dress until she had time to focus on how she was going to exact her revenge. As much as she was anxious to begin making Helena pay for what she did to Marie, her first priority was to care for her child. Sarah used the time it took to climb the stairs to her daughter's room to calm her anger to avoid detection.

When she spotted her daughter's, bloody body lying on her bed, everything in Sarah's body went numb; and when she spotted Helena in the room as well, she fought back the urge to slit her open navel to nose. Sensing that her presence may not be a good idea, Helena left the room; and Sarah began gently washing the blood from her daughter's back. The salve Sarah made would heal her daughter's physical scars, but the scars on her soul would be eternal.

Chapter Four

Revenge is a Dish Best Served Cold

Summer 1856

The wedding day had finally arrived, and Helena had long forgotten about the night she took her anger out on Marie. However, that night was forever seared into the memory of her future husband; and most of all in the memory of Marie's mother. The latter of which, had begun exacting revenge that very next morning. Knowing Helena's fondness for blackberries and that she used this as a reason to torture her daughter, Sarah thought it only fitting that she uses it to give Helena her ""Just Desserts" so to speak.

Every morning since that fateful night, Sarah prepared biscuits for breakfast; and she always made sure that Helena's included blackberry preserves. It never occurred to Helena to question why Sarah had suddenly gone through the trouble of making special preserves just for her, in fact, in her deluded mind she even thought that it was Sarah's way of trying to get on her good side. Helena was certain that Sarah knew that at any given time she could have her daughter killed or sold away to

Winston Dubois. So, she thought that making a preserve especially for her was a sort of peace offering for her daughter's inappropriate behavior. Helena had no idea, the preserves she was consuming contained more than just her favorite berries; and peace was the farthest thing from Sarah's mind.

The morning of her wedding, Helena ate her usual breakfast, including the special preserves. She floated around the house appearing to be on cloud nine as she prepared for her big day. Marie did her best to stay out of Helena's way and Sarah made sure that she, not Marie, was at Helena's beck and call. Sarah took great pleasure in watching Helena prepare to be John's wife and future mother of his children; not because she was celebrating her Mistress' happiness, but because she knew there was one dream Helena had that would never come true.

Being a slave meant that most people viewed them as they would a piece of furniture or one of their animals; so, they spoke freely around them. This practice was what gave Sarah all the information she needed to avenge her daughter. She knew that the Devereux and Marchand patriarchs needed an heir born from their children's union, and that Helena hoped that giving John a child would at least endear him to her.

From that information Sarah devised a plan to feed Helena a special preserve, made from her favorite berries and a few extra ingredients. The spell Sarah cast would mask the symptoms of the disease growing in Helena's body, until she was rendered barren, ensuring that she would never be able to produce life outside of her own.

Helena was finally dressed and ready to go meet her groom. She took one final approving look at herself in the mirror, before hurrying outside to the elaborate coach waiting to take her to the church. Helena arrived amidst a grand precession. This was the biggest affair New Orleans had ever seen. Heirs from two of the city's most affluent families were getting married. It was the social event of the year and all of New Orleans' elite were in full attendance. Helena and her mother soaked up all the attention, waving like royalty to those who crowded the streets for a glimpse of this self-appointed princess.

The coach pulled in front of the church and Helena stepped out. People cheered and waved as she ascended the stairs leading into the church escorted by her father. Helena's bridal party was dressed in blush pink dresses with elaborate beading around the bodice; and each carried a bouquet of roses of the same color. As she watched each of her bridesmaids make their way down the aisle, she was filled with excitement.

Turning to her father Helena said, "Oh daddy I can't believe this day's finally here! In just a few moments I'm going to walk down that aisle and become Mrs. John Devereux."

Pleased that his daughter's dream wedding was also going to make him even wealthier than he was before, Alexander Marchand felt almost as excited as his daughter.

"This is just the beginning my angel, you are going to get everything you deserve." Alexander said, while kissing his daughter's cheek.

The organist began to play to signal the bride's entrance. As John watched Helena come down the aisle, he imagined that it was Marie. He was so engrossed in his daydream that soon a genuine smile emerged on his face. Seeing John smiling at her in that manner made Helena's heart flutter and she began to think he was beginning to see her in a different light.

When she was finally standing in front of him and the priest began the vows, the mention of her name broke his trance and who he was really marrying came into focus. As quickly as it came, the smile faded from John's face adding yet another dagger in Helena's heart. She tried to appear unfazed as they both went through the formalities of the ceremony.

When it was over, the unhappy couple made their way down the aisle amongst well-wishers and exited to the carriage that was to take them to their reception. Once inside and out of earshot of the crowd, Helena turned to her husband and said, "When I walked down the aisle and saw you smiling at me, I thought you were finally seeing me as your wife."

Turning to face her with stoic expression, John replied, "When you saw me smiling I was imagining that Marie was walking towards me to become my wife. And when you saw my smile fade away that was when I saw you as my wife."

Helena felt like her heart was being ripped out of her chest. She had loved him for so long and being his wife was a symbol of her dream coming true. She would do anything for him, including risk her own life and nothing she did seemed to make any difference to him. It was as if he was under some spell cast by Marie and nothing she did could break it.

Desperate to make her marriage into the fairy tale she had dreamed it would be, Helena pleaded, "John, we are husband and wife now, can't you at least try to be happy with me? Ever since we were children, I knew we were destined to be together."

Having no sympathy for Helena's feelings or farfetched fantasies, John laughed and said, "Sweetheart, let's be clear on where we stand. We are pawns in our fathers' game of chess; and we are husband and wife in name only. To answer your question, I'll never be happy married to you. Ever since we were children I knew that I loved Marie, but I also knew that society would never allow us to be together; so, I'll have to love her from afar. But make no mistake, you may have my last name, but Marie will always have my heart. We are not destined to be together Helena, we are sentenced to be together; and I look forward to my life with you as I would life in prison."

With that, John turned away to look out the window and let his mind wander to thoughts of Marie. Helena sat quietly beside him with thoughts of Marie as well. She decided right then and there that if she was ever to win John's heart she must first eliminate the competition; but how? She would love nothing more than to watch her hanging from a tree or devoured by wild animals. She even had daydreams of slitting her throat herself and watching her bleed to death at her feet, but she knew none of those were realistic.

Killing Marie would only bring wrath from both John and her new father-in-law and that would surely not serve her well. So, she thought it was time to make good on the threat she made to sell Marie to Winston Dubois; but she knew she would have to be very careful how she carried out her plan. No one could know that she sold her; John would have to think she ran away. Helena spent the rest of the carriage ride and most of her reception perfecting her plan to get rid of Marie, and she knew she had to do it soon.

Instead of spending their time lost in marital bliss on the night of their wedding; John was drowning his sorrows in a bottle of whiskey and Helena was plotting her next move. She had slipped a note to Winston Dubois whom she had secretly invited to show up to their reception. When he arrived at the closed reception with no invitation, he was promptly asked to leave. Helena feigning disgust that someone of Winston's lower class would have the audacity to show up at her reception, confronted him.

While playing her role like an award-winning actress, Helena had stormed up to Winston and demanded that he leave at once. While seeming to shove him for effect, she slipped him the note asking that he meet her at the edge of the Devereux garden at midnight.

Once John was in a drunken stupor, Helena slipped out of the house to meet Winston. Careful not to wake anyone else, she tiptoed out of the house and made her way to the garden. "Winston," Helena whispered.

Winston, who spotted Helena as she entered the garden, stepped out from the shadows startling her so badly she almost stumbled.

"You nearly scared me to death!" Helena spat as she struggled to regain her composure.

"My...My Mrs. Devereux, you certainly are jumpy for a new bride," Winston said with a smirk.

Not amused, Helena retorted "Never mind about my marital status, we're here to discuss other business. I am prepared to give you something that I know you've wanted for a long time."

Curious as to what Helena was offering, Winston replied, "Is that so? And just what would that be?"

With a steady gaze, Helena answered, "Marie Jean Baptiste."

Knowing that Helena harbored a long standing resentment towards Marie for her place in John's heart, Winston knew why she wanted to get rid of Marie; but he also knew that their meeting in secret meant that John wasn't privy to this proposed transaction.

"Not that I'm not pleased to be acquiring a fine wench like Marie, but I have to inquire what prompted this sudden change of heart by the Devereuxs. She was never available for sale before under any circumstances. What changed?" Winston quizzed.

Tiring of Winston's games, Helena retorted, "Do you want to conduct an interview or purchase a slave?"

Sensing that pushing the matter may close his window of opportunity, Winston tabled his questions on why Marie was now for sale and simply asked how much she wanted for her.

"Six hundred dollars," Helena stated with no hesitation.

"Deal," Winston replied and pulled the sum from his pocket immediately.

Helena took the money and stuffed it in her dress. She saw Winston eyeing her breasts as she concealed her ill- gotten gains.

"You best keep your eyes to yourself sir, I am a married woman." Helena stated.

With a laugh, Winston replied, "Yes, but just like your husband, I only have eyes for Marie. Now, you make sure you get her to me before week's end; or I will be by to collect her myself."

Helena's eyes showed that she was displeased with both Winston's comments about Marie and his threat of exposing her deeds. Once again, a man would choose a slave over her. The consistent rejection by the male persuasion was starting to wear on Helena's fragile ego. How embarrassing was it that someone of such low stature would still rather have a common slave girl instead of someone of her status.

Angrily, Helena spat, "You will have your wench, but you will do well not to threaten me."

With stoic expression, Winston simply replied "Oh Mrs. Devereux, I think you know I never make threats."

Not wanting to prolong the conversation any further, Helena turned without another word and hurried back to the house. She wanted to sneak back in before anyone noticed that she was gone. John was in an alcohol induced coma and wouldn't be the wiser, but as Helena entered the house quiet as a mouse and made her way to her room seemingly undetected, she didn't even notice Sarah was standing there in the shadows...watching.

Chapter Five

Hell, hath no fury…

Helena walked around in deep thought for the remainder of the week. She wasn't pondering how to entice her new husband's heart, but rather trying to eliminate the woman who held it. Blinded by jealousy and rage, she was oblivious to the impending catastrophe that she had set in motion.

Helena had ignored the warnings she received from her new husband and father-in-law about allowing her emotions to control her actions; and the silent yet very deadly threat that Marie's mother Sarah posed. Instead, she was consumed with how she was going to get Marie   to Winston before the end of the week; and how she was going to convince everyone that Marie ran away.

Meanwhile, it was becoming increasingly hard to hide the fact that Marie was with child; a fact for which Peter Devereux had already began devising a plan. He knew that Marie's pregnancy would draw a lot of suspicion; and he couldn't handle the scandal of his newly married son siring   a bastard with the house slave. He had finally set his plan of fusing the Devereux and Marchand families' money and power together; and Marie's baby did not fit into his plans…at least not initially. Peter knew that Thomas Childress, another house slave, had always been fond of Marie, but he also knew that she did not return Thomas' interests. Unfortunately for her, Marie's feelings for Thomas made no difference to Peter. At the end of the day she was still a slave and she must obey her master.

Peter approached Thomas and informed him that he wanted him to marry Marie and take responsibility for the child she was carrying. It did not take a lot of convincing for Thomas to agree and it wasn't because he wanted to please his master; it was because like Helena, he was willing to accept anything to have the object of his affection.

Now that Thomas was given his directive on what Peter expected of him, Peter took him to find Marie. Marie was in the kitchen preparing lunch when she saw Peter enter with Thomas. She felt a sinking feeling in the pit of her stomach; and she knew whatever was coming next was not going to be good.

"Marie I'm not going to waste time trying to sugar coat this, because judging by the looks of your belly you are going to be a mother any day. Now we just have to work out the pesky detail of who your child's father will be," Peter said, looking at a now pale Marie. Noticing that Marie was now white as a sheet and appearing faint, Peter continued. "Oh no need to bother trying to hide it from me darling, I know you are carrying my son's child."

Fear gripped Marie's body. She knew how much Helena hated her; and she figured that if Master Devereux had figured it out, so had Helena. Getting to the point of his visit, Peter ushered Thomas forward. "Now Marie, I think you know that no one can know that my son is the father of that baby; and as pretty as you are, I am also sure you are not the Virgin Mary, so Immaculate Conception can't explain how you became with child. That is where Thomas comes in."

Marie felt that feeling in the pit of her stomach growing as she had begun to realize, just what Master Devereux was saying. Once he saw that Marie had started to catch on, Peter continued, "You and Thomas are going to get married, and he is going to raise your child as his very own. Obviously, time is of the essence, so the ceremony will be tomorrow."

Knowing that she had no say in the decision, she just cast her eyes down to the floor and replied, "Yes Master Devereux."

Pleased that he had gotten his only perceived loose end successfully tied, Peter left to tend to other matters. "I'll leave you two love birds alone to get acquainted," Peter stated as he exited the kitchen.

Left alone with the man she was being forced to marry, Marie neither spoke nor even looked up. She feared if she did, she would start to cry and never stop.

News of Marie and Thomas' impending nuptials spread across the plantation like wildfire. And was music to Helena's ears. Now she didn't have to worry about selling her to Winston, allowing her to stay would afford Helena the opportunity to enjoy Marie's suffering. Knowing that Marie was being forced to marry a man she didn't love made Helena's evil heart rejoice.

Helena also reveled in the thought that while Marie's child was a blood heir to the Devereux fortune, it would never be more than a slave, and Helena's children would be their masters. The thought brought a huge smile to her face. That was until she remembered that she had sold Marie to Winston; and tomorrow would not only be Marie's wedding day, but also the deadline for delivering her to Winston. Now Helena had to figure out how she was going to break her deal with Winston, without exposing that she made a deal with the devil in the first place.

That night Marie cried herself to sleep, but she wasn't the only one dreading the next day. Helena lay awake in her bed thinking of how she was going to convince Winston to give up Marie and not tell anyone that she sold her in the first place. Winston had set his sights on Marie when she was 12 years old, but Peter refused to sell her. Since that time, he had periodically tried to convince Peter to reconsider, but he was always met with a resounding and emphatic no.

Convincing Winston to give Marie up now that he finally had her, seemed like an insurmountable task; but she had to try. What is it about that damn slave girl that drives men to madness? Helena thought to herself, before finally falling asleep. She had a busy day ahead of her and if she was going to outsmart Winston and the Devereuxs, she was going to need a good night's sleep.

Morning arrived, and a weary Marie rose to bathe and dress for her wedding. This was a day that she and most women had always dreamed about; but in her dreams, she was marrying the man she loved, not someone she was forced to marry. Knowing that no amount of wishful thinking would change her fate, Marie tried to look at the positives. Thomas was a good man and she knew he would be a good father to her baby.

Looking down at her belly, she said, "Well it could be worse baby; we could have been sold to Master Dubois. At least the good Lord saw fit to spare us that fate." Marie rubbed her stomach in a comforting manner like she was trying to reassure her little one, and herself, that everything would be okay. Little did she know, the Lord may have seen fit to spare her that fate, but Helena did not; and before the end of the day, she would come face to face with the man she feared more than the devil.

Sarah came into her daughter's room carrying a dress she wore when she married Marie's father Nathaniel. They were young and very much in love. They were both slaves on a plantation in Shreveport, Louisiana; but when their Masters fell on hard times, they sold them all away. Nathaniel and their barely 3-year-old son Jacob were bought by a slave owner from North Carolina and Sarah was bought by the Devereuxs. She was 3 months pregnant with Marie at the time and her husband never got to hold the beautiful baby girl they had created; and Jacob never got to see his baby sister.

The day she arrived at the Devereux plantation, she placed the dress away in an old trunk along with her broken heart. She had always imagined that one day she would give it to Marie on her wedding day, but Sarah had hoped it would be for her daughter to marry the love of her life. When it became clear that John Devereux was the love of her daughter's life, she knew that would never happen. Now she hoped that wearing her dress, would give her the strength to get through tomorrow and the rest of her life.

"I have something for you baby," Sarah said as she laid the dress on Marie's bed.

Turning around to see her mother's wedding dress, Marie's eyes filled with tears. "Momma, that's the dress you married daddy in; I can't wear that. It wouldn't be right. That dress is a symbol of the love you had for daddy; I don't love Thomas. I won't sully daddy's memory like that." Marie said with tears now streaming down her face.

Feeling her own heart breaking, Sarah took Marie's face in her hands and whispered, "Shhh now baby. Don't cry. I know that marrying Thomas is not what you want to do, but it is a better option than what Ms. Helena had planned for you."

Marie's blood ran cold. She knew that Helena could be vicious when her ego was bruised; and Marie having John's baby would be a constant reminder to Helena of the night Marie had shared with her husband. Marie could only imagine what torturous punishment Helena had in store for her.

"What's she going to do to me momma?" Marie asked with a heart filled with dread and fear.

"Never you mind what crazy thoughts Miss. Helena got roaming around in that evil head of hers. She wouldn't dare do anything to you now. Master Devereux has her on a tight leash and just in case she manages to break free. I have just the thing to remind that bitch to stay in her own backyard." Sarah said, holding her daughter close.

Marie didn't know what Helena had planned, but she knew that she had made a dangerous enemy in Sarah. Marie managed to drag herself into the bath and began preparing to marry a man she didn't love, to protect the baby she loved more than life. She moved through the motions of getting dressed as if she was on autopilot. Her face absents of the joy most brides feel on their wedding day. Marie stood there, staring at herself in the mirror. The dress was beautiful, and her mother had let it out a bit to accommodate her growing belly.

Standing there, Marie tried to imagine that she was headed down to a grand ceremony to become Mrs. John Devereux. The thought brought a genuine smile to her face; and then she felt her mother's hands on her shoulders.

"Come on baby, its time." Sarah said, ushering her daughter down to the farce of a ceremony.

Marie felt her knees get weak and Sarah was literally holding her daughter up as she guided her outside to meet her groom.

When Marie crossed the threshold of the house and saw Thomas standing there waiting for her at the end of the porch, her mind started to accept what her heart still could not; she was about to marry a man she didn't love. Marie avoided looking at John because she didn't want to see the pain in his eyes; and she avoided looking at Helena to avoid the gleam of unmitigated joy in hers. Instead she decided to focus her attention where she could find the most strength; and amazingly it was right in front of her.

As she moved closer to Thomas, she tried to focus on   his face. He was a fair skinned man with bluish green eyes and hair that was a dark sandy brown color. He was average height, but his body was chiseled and well defined. He was an attractive man; and had her heart not belonged to another, she would probably have been happy to have him as a husband. Thomas was a good man with a kind heart; and she knew he would do all he could to take care of her and her baby. Those thoughts managed to bring a smile to Marie's face. Walking towards Thomas she saw in his eyes what every bride wants to see; an eternal, unwavering look of love.

Because Marie and Thomas were both house slaves, they had the benefit of having an actual ceremony; even though their marriage would still not be legally recognized. When Marie reached Thomas, she felt as if she was going to faint; her knees were weak and the butterflies in her stomach exacerbated the nausea she was already feeling. She felt like she was all alone in the center of a room full of mocking people taking pleasure in her despair. As if he could sense what she needed, Thomas took Marie's hand and squeezed it gently, as if to say, 'it's ok. I am here now; you will never be alone again.' Marie looked up into Thomas' eyes and found her strength.

There was an old plantation minister who was enlisted to marry the couple. When he began presiding over the ceremony; Marie had finally begun to feel like everything was going to be ok. Helena had become so caught up in watching Marie's visible discomfort that she had forgotten that there was a very problematic loose end that she forgot to tie up. None had noticed that an unexpected and uninvited guest was lurking in the wings.

The minister had gone through the vows without a hitch, but when he spoke the words "If there be anyone here who can show just cause why these two should not be married, let them speak now or forever hold their peace," everything changed. The uninvited guest was none other than Winston Dubois and he had come to claim his merchandise.

In a slow southern drawl, Winston said, "Why yes mister nigger minister sir, I can show just cause. You see this here gal is my slave and I did not give her permission to marry." Everyone turned to see Winston standing there with an evil grin.

Marie's blood ran cold and her heart was pounding in her chest, but she was not the only one startled by his presence. Helena turned white as a ghost and waited with bated breath to see if he was going to reveal how he came to own Marie. Winston moved in to grab Marie and on instinct, Thomas placed her behind him in a protective stance.

Finding it humorous that a slave would think that he   had the right to attempt to "protect" another slave from their master, Winston laughed and said, "And just what do you think you are doing boy? You can't keep me from taking this gal anywhere; now stand aside, before I have you horse whipped."

As Winston extended his hand to grab Marie he felt a sting on his wrist and watched in disbelief as his white shirt now turned a bright crimson red. Snatching his injured arm away, he turned to see Peter standing there with his knife still extended.

"Have you taken leave of your senses?" Winston quizzed while holding his wrist to stop the bleeding.

Without breaking his stare or removing his blade, Peter coolly responded, "No, but you shall take leave of your hand if you mistakenly attempt to place it where it doesn't belong again."

Not willing to give up Marie that easily, Winston barked. "This gal is my property! I paid six hundred dollars for her and I've come to retrieve my merchandise!"

With his blade still fixed on Winston, Peter turned his gaze to meet Helena's now frightened eyes and asked, "Now I know I never agreed to sell Marie to you, so with whom did you make this transaction?"

Helena felt as if her father in law's stare was burrowing a hole through her; and she visibly started shaking. Although she wanted to flee more than anything at that moment, she knew it was best that she not moves a muscle.

It came as no surprise that Winston named Helena as the one from whom he purchased Marie. Turning back to Winston, Peter said, "I apologize that you were mistakenly informed that Marie was for sale. My daughter-in-law will gladly return your money with an additional 50 dollars for your inconvenience."

Unsatisfied with Peter's offer, Winston retorted, "I don't want the money back or your petty bribe. I want my slave and I want her now!"

Moving in closer and allowing the tip of his blade to touch Winston's Adam's apple, Peter replied, "I would choose my next words carefully sir, for they may be your last. Now you have entered into a fraudulent transaction to purchase property that is not and will never be for sale. I suggest that you cut your losses and be happy that you are leaving with your money and your life."

Sensing that Peter was not going to waiver on his stance and that to further push the matter could prove fatal, Winston backed down. Peter's eyes remained fixed on Winston as he ordered Helena to retrieve her ill-gotten gains and return them to Winston. Like a scolded child, Helena cast her eyes to the floor and scurried off to get the money. Her heart was pounding in her chest, because she knew she had once again found herself on her father-in-law's bad side.

Helena was cursing herself for getting involved with someone of low class like Winston, she was certain it was his improper breeding that made him sell her out. When she returned she handed the money to Winston, but made sure that she did not make eye contact. In fact, she was sure not to make eye contact with anyone, especially John or Peter. If she could, she would melt into her chair and disappear for a while, because she was sure this was not going to end well for her down the line.

Winston conceded his immediate defeat, but warned, "You have just made a grave error in judgment Mr. Devereux; I am not an enemy you want to have."

Without flinching Peter responded, "Nor am I Mr. Dubois; and if you are not off my property in the next five seconds this day will mark both a wedding and a funeral." Without further incident, Winston turned and left. But Peter knew that this was not going to be the last time he   had to deal with his new enemy; and Helena knew that she would soon have to deal with Peter.

Chapter Six

What's Done in the Dark

Once Winston was gone and everyone regained their composure, the wedding continued. Marie's heart had returned to its normal rhythm and she had found a new fondness for Thomas in the wake of his earlier heroics. Placing himself in danger to protect her and her unborn child further solidified her feeling that Thomas would make a good husband and father.

When the ceremony was complete, everyone proceeded to the dining room for food and dance; which was another advantage of being a house slave. Although Marie's heart had not let go of John, she had made a little room for Thomas. Marie and Thomas laughed and danced while enjoying their reception. For a short time, the two could almost imagine their lives as free individuals…almost.

Everyone was enjoying the party, except John and Helena, for two very different reasons. John was exposed to the same pain that he imagined Marie felt watching him marry Helena. He attempted to drown his heartbreak in whisky, hoping it would dull the memory that he almost witnessed the woman he loved, and his unborn child being taken away by a sadistic rapist. He also wanted to forget that he was shackled in marriage to the woman who orchestrated the entire event.

The thought suddenly made John feel the need for some air, so he slipped away from the festivities to continue his pity party on the front porch. Helena would have normally taken this opportunity to try to get close to John, but she was no fool; and she knew that after Winston exposed her as the culprit in the sale of Marie, it was best that she keeps as low a profile as possible. But she could have been invisible and that would not have saved her from the wrath she would face from Peter and most of all, from Sarah.

Helena's latest little stunt had prompted Sarah to intensify the spell she had already cast on her. Originally Sarah was just going to make Helena suffer the embarrassment of her little fling causing her to be barren, but now she wanted Helena to suffer physical anguish as well.

While the guests were dancing and feasting the day away, Sarah was making a brand-new potion for the new Mrs. Devereux. When she finished she had a fine white powder that she mixed into a glass of champagne. As she approached Helena with the glass, Sarah bore a genuine smile that hid her deadly intent.

"I brought you some champagne Mrs. Devereux," Sarah said, handing the glass to Helena.

"But I didn't ask for anything," Helena replied, looking surprised.

"I know, but you look as if you could use it Miss. Mr. Dubois showing up like that putting you at odds with Master Devereux couldn't have been easy for you. I thought that after what happened today, you deserved this drink, sorry if I overstepped Mistress." Sarah said in an apologetic tone.

"No, you were right, I could use a drink after all; thank you Sarah," Helena said, taking the drink from Sarah's hand.

Feigning a humble bow, Sarah replied, "It was my pleasure Mistress." Helena downed the champagne and returned the glass to Sarah.

"I am going to retire to my quarters Sarah. This day has taken a lot out of me." Helena turned to go to her bedroom.

Sarah nodded in acknowledgement while thinking, I have just begun to take from you, you evil shrew! When I'm done, the fires of hell will seem like a vacation.

Helena entered her room and began to feel faint. She thought it was because of the heat and decided to remove her clothing and lay down. Soon she drifted off to sleep, but it was not a peaceful slumber. Almost immediately Helena's body felt paralyzed and she could not move. She dreamed that she was being held down by some invisible force and burned alive. The pain was excruciating, yet she could not cry out and she could not wake up.

Helena lay in this hell like place with no escape or relief from her suffering until the next morning. When she awoke, she was sweating and gasping for breath. John, who slept on the chaise in their bedroom, looked at Helena and said, "Are you ill? You look almost as horrible outside as you really are inside."

Catching her breath and smoothing her wet red hair back from her face; Helena replied, "I had the most horrible nightmare. I felt like I was in hell being burned alive, but I could not cry out for help. It was horrible."

With a smirk, John replied, "Darling, wherever you are, is hell," and took a drink from a freshly poured glass of whiskey.

Turning her attention to John, she replied, "Don't you think it's a little early to be drinking?"

Downing the glass' contents John responded, "The devil himself would need a drink to stand being in your presence! I always knew you were a miserable bitch, but yesterday you surpassed even my low expectations of you. You are disturbed because you dreamed you were in hell? Sweetheart, hell is too good for you; and apparently the devil agrees, seeing as how he sent your vile carcass back to torture us with your presence."

Looking appalled, Helena spat, "You wish that I would have a nightmarish sleep?"

John moved so close to Helena that she could smell the whiskey and feel the heat of his breath touching her face and whispered, "I don't wish that you would have a nightmarish sleep; I wish you would die in your sleep and end my nightmare of being your husband."

As he turned to exit the room, Helena cried out, "I love you John; I would do anything to make you happy! All I've done has been so that we can have a happy life together!"

John stopped in his tracks and without even turning around, said, "Do you truly mean that? Would you do anything to make me happy?"

Thinking her declaration had gained her favor, she excitedly responded, "Yes my darling, I would do anything. Tell me what you want me to do."

John turned around and went to Helena. He gently took her hands in his and looked deep into her eyes. "If you truly want to make me happy my sweet, when you go to bathe this morning, take something of mine into the bath with you."

Happily, intrigued, Helena asked, "What would you like me to take my darling?"

John gently pushed her hair from her ear and holding her head in his hand he whispered, "While you are lying there in that nice warm bath, I want you to take my razor and slit your wrists."

Disturbed by his comments, Helena tried to pull away, but John's gentle grip had suddenly become firm as he continued. "If you truly want to make me and everyone else happy you will kill yourself. Think of it as saving the world; because not having your miserable ass in it, will truly make this world a better place".

John then released his grip and left the room. Helena fell to the floor and sobbed uncontrollably, but no one came to her aid. After what seemed like hours, Helena pulled herself up from the floor and ordered one of the servants to draw her bath. Sarah came to Helena's room to prepare her bath. Not wanting anyone, including any of the slaves to see her in such a disheveled state, Helena did not have

Sarah stay to add the touches of fragrant salts and lavender water to her bath; today she would do that herself. But Sarah had already added her own special touches to Helena's bath. The fine white powder that she mixed in her champagne, she had also mixed in Helena's lavender water.

Helena stripped off her wrinkled clothing and pinned her long red hair atop her head. She submerged herself in the water and let its warmth comfort her like a lover's embrace. Just as she had the night before, Helena drifted off into a deep coma like sleep. This time she felt as if she was drowning. She felt the pain of the water expanding her lungs to the point it felt as if they would burst. Paralysis again gripped her body. She couldn't move to save herself and she couldn't breathe. Panic began to set in as her mind was telling her limbs to move, but they would not.

When she finally awoke, she frantically climbed from the tub landing on the floor. She scurried to the corner of the room grabbing a towel to cover her.

Helena sat shivering and looking at the tub like a watery grave in which she was almost placed. She felt like she was losing her mind, but convinced herself that it was just the stress that she'd been under the last few weeks. After she calmed down and managed to get dressed. She decided she would take a walk in the garden to clear her mind. Along the way, she noticed Thomas and Marie outside. Thomas was placing his hand on Marie's stomach to feel the baby move; and Marie was donning a big smile and motherly glow. The way Thomas looked at Marie was the same way that John did; and the way she wished he would look at her just once.

Why in the hell is he so happy to feel another man's baby moving in his wife's belly? And why after all I have done, to wipe that smug smile off that uppity nigger bitch's face is she still happy? Helena thought to herself as she stared at the happy newlyweds.

Even though Marie was now no threat to her marriage to John and had seemingly accepted her fate as Thomas' wife, it enraged Helena that Marie was still so happy. It was not enough for her that Marie wasn't with the love of her life; Helena had a sadistic need to see Marie broken. Her fixation on Marie was so strong, that Helena had pushed her recent hellish experiences to the recesses of her mind, but Sarah was nowhere close to being done with her; and she would give Helena plenty of opportunities to reflect on her own suffering.

Feeling that Marie had ruined her plans to clear her head, Helena returned to the house for the breakfast she skipped earlier that morning. Maybe if I get some food in my stomach, I will feel better. She thought, as she made her way back into the house. Still consumed with thoughts of Marie, Helena sat down at the kitchen table in an almost trance like state.

"Are you alright Mistress; can I make you something to eat?" Sarah said, as she walked over to Helena.

Snapping out of her trance, Helena replied, "Yes Sarah, I am absolutely famished. I would like two eggs over easy, toast and some of that blackberry jam you made."

Happy to oblige, Helena's request to consume more of her 'special jam', Sarah responded, "Right away Mistress."

Sarah served Helena her breakfast, then excused herself to attend to other household chores; which included adding a little something extra to Helena's pillow cases and bed sheets. The weeks rolled on and every night Helena was plagued with disturbing dreams and sleep paralysis; but now instead of her anguish and physical torment being confined only to her dreams, they were now manifesting themselves in real life.

After awakening from one of her nightmares which involved her body breaking out in painful boils, Helena noticed a cluster of small boils had begun to form on the side of her face near her ear. She attempted to treat the problem with a salve made from aloe and eucalyptus and submerged herself in a bath of her fragrant salts and lavender water. Helena figured that the boils were a sign that she was fatigued and stressed, so she thought a relaxing bath would help calm her nerves.

As she tried to clear her mind and focus on the feeling of the warm water on her skin, Helena drifted off to sleep. This time it was a peaceful one, with no paralysis or bad dreams. When she awoke, she felt refreshed and in better spirits. Thinking that her unfortunate run of nightmares was now over, Helena emerged from her bath with a huge smile and sigh of relief. She grabbed a towel and wrapped it around her body. When the towel touched her skin, she felt intense pain.

When Helena opened the towel, and looked at herself in the mirror she noticed that her entire body was now covered in the painful and unsightly boils. She pulled her hair back to look at the cluster that was on the side of her face and noticed that not only had it begun to spread; but when she pulled her hand away she was holding a large patch of red hair. Frantic Helena ran her hands through her hair and each time she removed handfuls of red curls. She screamed so loud that both slaves and members of the Devereux family all ran into the bedroom to see what was wrong.

They arrived to see a completely naked Helena standing in the mirror crying and screaming; with piles of red hair at her feet and large puss filled boils covering her body. The sight was so ghastly it defied belief, not to mention that a foul odor was also starting to emit from her body. Sarah, who was among those who entered the room, rushed to Helena's aid and covered her in a bed sheet she ripped from the bed. "Hush now Mistress, everything is going to be all right. I'm going to take care of you," Sarah said with feigned concern.

Inside she was quite pleased with how well her potion was ravaging Helena's body. Helena screamed in pain as the bed sheets felt like razor blades against her skin. Peter Devereux ordered John to get the family doctor to come to the house right away. It took John a minute to gain enough composure to do as he was asked; he had begun to vomit from the site and smell of his wife, but managed to collect himself and head into town.

In the meantime, Sarah played the role of the dutiful concerned slave and tended to Helena. She wiped her sweaty brow and even hummed a soothing tune for good measure. Peter ordered everyone out of the room and left only Sarah to look after an ailing Helena. Sarah stared into the face of her victim. Helena's skin once beautiful and smooth as cream, was now riddled with putrid smelling boils. Her fiery red locks once her crown and glory now lay in patches on the floor. She was enduring such suffering that she resembled a wounded animal; and Sarah almost felt bad for her…almost.

It seemed like an eternity passed before Dr. Sinclair arrived, but once he did he ushered everyone out of them room so that he could examine Helena. Her condition perplexed him, and he had no idea what to do for her, so he gave her a sedative to at least relieve her suffering while he tried to figure it out.

Dr. Sinclair examined Helena from head to toe. When he noticed that the boils were most concentrated in her vaginal area, he discovered at least one problem; Helena had contracted gonorrhea. It was one of the worst cases he had ever seen, and it appeared to have manifested itself in the form of these ghastly boils that spread all over her body. After completing a vaginal exam, Dr. Sinclair went outside to give the Devereuxs the news.

"Ok Dr. Sinclair, give it to me straight. What the hell is wrong with her? I have never seen anything like that in my life! Did she have some sort of allergic reaction to something?" Peter asked upon seeing the doctor emerge from Helena's room.

"Well she is apparently having a reaction, but it's not to something; it's to someone." Dr. Sinclair responded debating on how to deliver the news.

Looking visibly perplexed, Peter quizzed, "Someone? What the hell are you trying to say doc? This girl broke out like a goddamn leper 'cause she got too close to someone?"

Still trying to choose his words carefully, Dr. Sinclair replied, "In a manner of speaking." The doctor looked around as if he was searching for the best way to reveal his discovery. He knew that the Devereuxs were a prominent family and held in high regard, so he wanted to handle the situation as delicately as possible.

Not being in the mood to play guessing games, Peter retorted, "Damn it doc, I didn't bring you out here to play a rousing game of name that affliction! What the hell's wrong with her? I've seen a lot of things in my life Doc and some of them I would rather gouge my eyes out than see again; and seeing Helena lying in there looking like a damn monster from a bad nightmare is one of them! Now I'm going to ask you this one more time and I swear if you don't give me a straight answer, you'll be laying up in a damn bed right beside her."

Sensing that tact was no longer an option, Dr. Sinclair replied. "Mr. Devereux, your daughter in law has contracted gonorrhea."

Peter along with everyone else stood silent, astonished at the news; everyone but Sarah. Snapping back to reality, Peter replied, "I'm sorry doctor, did you just say that Helena has gonorrhea?"

Solemnly, Dr. Sinclair replied, "Yes; and it's the worst case I have ever seen."

Turning his attention to John, Peter said, "Son we have to have the doc check you out immediately!"

Interrupting his father before he could continue his speech or imply that he had somehow infected Helena, John responded, "Now hold on father; someone definitely needs to be checked out, but it's not me. I have never been anywhere near Helena; and given the news we just received from the good doctor here, I think I made the right choice. Now I don't know who Helena has been rolling in the hay with, but it sure as hell wasn't me! This just goes to show you father. Being a whore surpasses class and breeding."

Now opting for full disclosure, Dr. Sinclair detailed the extent of Helena's infection; and the harm it had done to her body. He informed the Devereuxs that, so much time had passed without treatment, that the disease had done irreparable damage that was so extensive that Helena would never be able to carry a child. The disease had left her sterile and destroyed any hopes Peter had of a child being born of John and Helena's union.

Chapter Seven

If You Can't be With the One You Love…

Fall 1856

Although they were in the house at the time, Marie and Thomas were not present for the drama that was unfolding concerning Helena. They were too busy adjusting to being newlyweds and preparing for the baby.

After they were married, the couple was allowed to move together into one of the larger rooms to accommodate them and the baby. Marie had been having some pains that evening and was allowed to rest in her room; and her new husband was taking care of her.

Although she and Thomas grew up together on the Devereux plantation and had known each other all of their lives, Marie felt as if she was meeting a stranger. Thomas knew everything about Marie, because he paid attention to every detail where she was concerned. He had loved her for such a long time that it was only natural for him to learn what makes her happy and what makes her sad.

Marie had never looked at Thomas as anything more than a friend, so some things about him she never noticed before; like what a beautiful smile he had and how kind his eyes were. She never noticed how handsome he was or how fit. His chiseled frame had gone unnoticed and covered in a uniform all those years. She never knew how strong he was or the gentleness of his touch. Her ears had never given recognition to his gifted singing voice or the fact that he had a wonderful sense of humor.

Although their marriage was one of convenience for their Master, it afforded Marie the opportunity to learn these things about her new husband.

While most newlyweds can't wait to enjoy the physical pleasures of their spouse after they are married, Thomas knew that Marie did not share those same desires for him. He had dreamed of making love to Marie for a long time, but he would never force her into a situation where she was uncomfortable. Instead he used this as an opportunity to show Marie that even though he wasn't John Devereux, he was a good man who would love her the way she should be loved; and give her the opportunity to develop feelings for him in return in her own time.

On their wedding night, Thomas entertained Marie with funny stories and beautiful songs. He had a melodious voice that could soothe a troubled mind; and his stories made Marie's face hurt from smiling. She had never remembered laughing so much in her life. She even found herself imagining him sitting in the old rocking chair in their room, rocking the baby to sleep with lullabies and magical stories. Although theirs was not a typical wedding night for newlyweds, for Marie and Thomas it was even more special. They spent the night talking and learning all about each other.

Finally, when Marie fell asleep in his arms that night; she felt she was in the safest place in the world. Over the next couple of months Marie found herself becoming fonder of her new husband with each passing day. He was very attentive to her needs and was as excited about her baby's arrival as she was. He had spent hours of his time at night working on a beautiful handmade bassinette for the baby; and would sing and talk to Marie's stomach. Marie and her mother Sarah would spend time knitting and sowing blankets and clothing for the expected bundle of joy. Even though there wasn't an official baby shower for slaves, the men and women were all using what they could to fashion toys or other gifts for Marie and the baby.

When Thomas had finished the bassinette, Marie had made a pillow like mattress to place in the bottom and a blanket to keep the baby warm. They marveled at how well they had worked together to make a comfortable place for their little one to sleep. That night, Marie fell asleep in her husband's arms and dreamed of the day when her baby would be asleep beside them in their beautiful new bed.

The next morning, November 1, 1856, Marie awoke to sharp pains and cramping in her belly; and Thomas awoke to wet sheets. During the night, Marie's water broke; and she was now in labor. The day had finally arrived when she would meet the little person inside her belly that had caused such a stir. After making sure Marie was lying comfortably in the bed, Thomas raced out of the room to tell everyone the baby was coming. Sarah rushed to her daughter's side with the plantation midwife in tow.

Marie's screams were so loud they could be heard throughout the house. Helena, who was still recovering in her room, also heard the sounds signaling the birth of her husband's child. The only heir to the Devereux throne was to be born from a slave; the thought alone was more painful than the horrible boils that still plagued her body. Although Sarah had released her grip on Helena, it still took some time for her to completely heal.

John had also heard Marie's screams and his heart leapt with joy for the new life that was created from their love; then broke in two because he would never get to raise his child or teach them any of the things he dreamed he would one day get to pass along. And now that Helena was no longer able to have any children, John gave up any hope of ever having that chance. As much as he wanted to be in the room with Marie while she gave birth to their child, he knew that was not his place; so, he went to the front porch where he could pray for his child and its mother in peace.

Meanwhile inside the house, Marie's labor was in full swing. "I feel like this baby is ripping me in two!" Marie screamed as she held Thomas' hand and pushed as she was instructed by the midwife.

"You got to push chile!" The old midwife said with a thick African accent.

Marie gritted her teeth and bore down to push. Sarah wiped her daughter's brow with a cool cloth;

but it wasn't her mother or the midwife that Marie looked to for strength, it was Thomas. It was Thomas' hand that she gripped for support and his eyes that she looked into for reassurance.

"It's a boy!" the midwife said raising the baby up for the parents to see and allowing Thomas to cut the cord.

Marie collapsed onto the bed from exhaustion and Sarah took the baby to clean him up. Just when Marie thought it was over, she felt another sharp pain rip through her body.

"What's happening? What's wrong? Why is it still hurting?" Marie asked between groans of pain. Everyone in the room had the same question; and they all began praying that nothing was wrong. The old midwife looked between Marie's legs to see another baby's head crowning.

"You having another baby chile" she said preparing Marie to deliver the second baby.

"What? No, I can't do it! I don't have the strength left!"
Marie cried.

"You can do it baby. You are the strongest woman I know; and you are strong enough to bring both of our babies into this world. Now squeeze my hand and push. I'm right here with you. We gonna get through this together; now push!" Thomas said, holding Marie's hand.

Marie mustered up enough strength to push until the second baby boy was safely delivered. Once the second baby was cleaned up, Sarah and the Midwife handed the babies to an excited Thomas and an exhausted Marie. It didn't take long for everyone to notice that these twins were very different. The first one born was light in complexion but obviously a black child. It had features that resembled the mother and dark black curly hair. The second baby didn't look black at all. His features resembled those of his father; and he had Lilly white skin, blue eyes and sandy blonde hair. If everyone had not witnessed him come through Marie's birth canal you would not know it was a black baby.

While everyone stood silently astonished, Peter entered the room to check on Marie and the baby. It also didn't take him long to notice the disparity between the two babies.

"Congratulations Thomas and Marie; it seems you were doubly blessed," Peter said, while thinking that this strange twist of fate could be the answer to his prayers.

Marie and Thomas simultaneously replied, "Thank you Master Devereux" as if they were singing in chorus. Marie didn't know what was going through Peter's mind, but the look in his eyes sent chills down her spine.

Peter excused himself from the room so that he couldfocus on the new ideas that were now running through his mind like a wildfire. This new baby could be the answer to my prayers! Marie and Thomas could keep the Black twin and raise him as planned; and John and Helena could take the White twin and raise him as the heir that everyone is expecting! Helena's recent illness could provide the plausible cover I need to explain the unexpected birth. She had been confined to the house for the last two months and no one was allowed to visit her, so no one outside of the family knows the reason for her sickness. Peter plotted.

As he was walking his mind kept scheming. We could say that we kept the pregnancy a secret because the doctors didn't know if the baby was going to make it and Helena was placed on strict bed rest. Since John is actually the father it won't technically be a lie and I will have a blood heir to secure my legacy! Peter contemplated as he went to find his son to share the news. He was so excited and pleased with himself, that he was almost giddy. Now he just had to bring everyone else up to speed and he could set his plan in motion.

Marie and Thomas had gotten over the shock of the additional baby and the unexpected complexion. Thomas lay in the bed with Marie as they held their new sons in their arms. "What are we going to name them?" Thomas asked.

Marie looked at the darker twin and said, "I think this one should be named Thomas Childress Jr; and this one we could name Timothy Childress"

A huge smile spread across Thomas' face and he leaned down and gave Marie a kiss on the lips. It was the first real kiss they had ever shared, and it was the softest Marie had ever felt. Once the twins were asleep, Thomas put them both in the bassinette, so Marie could rest. Sarah stayed with her to help tend to the little ones and Thomas went to start working on a second bassinette. He enlisted the help of some of the other men and worked through the night. By morning, both twins had their very own beds.

Thomas quietly placed the new bassinette in the room with both twins' beds side by side. The women had worked to make another soft pillow like bedding for the new twin as well. Thomas placed Timothy in his new bed, and then stared down at his sons sleeping so soundly. He had never remembered being so happy before; and he couldn't wait to see Marie's face when she awoke and saw the new bed. He was exhausted from working through the night, so he lay down beside Marie and drifted off into a peaceful slumber. Sarah gave the new parents some privacy, but stayed close so she could help when she was needed.

Meanwhile Peter had found his son and presented him with an update on Marie and her unexpected addition; as well as his plan for the 'Bonus Child'. John thought his father's plan was insane and didn't want to go along with it; but Peter Devereux was not the type of man to take no for an answer and his charm was unmatched in any arena. Peter wooed John with thoughts of not only being able to fulfill his dream of raising a biological son of his own, but also having the opportunity to raise a child created from his love with Marie. He would be able to freely love and groom this child, giving him the life he always wanted.

Once Peter got John to look at the plan from that perspective, he rationalized that he would be honoring Marie and their love by giving at least one of their children the life they deserved. With John on board, Peter just had to break the news to the new parents. He decided to wait a while to do that; now that his plan was devised, he could take a little time to set it in motion.

Tucked away in what seemed like their own little world, Thomas and Marie were enjoying being parents. Marie was so in love with her sons and not just because they were a part of her and John. Thomas was beyond proud. No one would ever know that it was not his blood running through their little veins. He was up every time either child even whimpered.

Sometimes Marie would wake, and Thomas would be sitting in the rocking chair with a baby in each arm, lovingly rocking them to sleep with a melodious lullaby; or telling them beautiful stories about a land and a time where they could be anything they wanted. His stories were always set in Africa and were a mixture of stories his own mother (who was African) used to tell him as a boy. Sometimes the characters were royals, sometimes they would be tradesmen, but they were always free men and women.

Marie loved those moments and her feelings for Thomas were growing each day. He was a good man and he lived to make her happy; but as happy as she was being a new mother and a new wife, Marie had an underlying sinking feeling that something bad was coming. She felt that feeling ever since she saw the look in Peter Devereux's eyes when he first saw the twins. Marie couldn't put her finger on it, but she knew she didn't like it. There was something sinister lurking behind his smile and congratulatory remarks to the new parents. The words on the surface appeared appropriate and genuine, but they still made the hairs on the back of Marie's neck stand up. Call it instinct or mother's intuition; but whatever it was, Marie's internal alarm was signaling that her happiness was about to be short lived.

Marie wasn't the only one that picked up on the strange vibes in the air. Peter was going through the motions of his normal routines, but there was an eerie calmness about him that was obvious to everyone around him. Helena had noticed it as well, but given her recent bout with her very deadly yet unexplainable sickness, her father-in-law's demeanor was the least of her concerns. John also noticed his father's mood change, but he knew the cause; and although part of him knew that what his father was proposing was reprehensible, it was overshadowed by the thought of being able to raise at least one of the children he fathered with Marie.

Since, Marie's marriage to Thomas, John's already questionable drinking habits worsened. He began spending so much time with a bottle of whiskey; Helena commented that it had replaced Marie as his mistress. It was times like this that John missed his mother. Elizabeth Devereux or "Lizzie" as his father affectionately called her, the most. After all, she was the heart and soul of the Devereux family; and her passing left a void that was never quite filled.

Peter loved Elizabeth beyond reason. They were childhood sweethearts and she always managed to bring out the softer more humane side of him. When John was five years old Elizabeth died from pneumonia and a piece of Peter died with her; the best piece. Since then, he has managed to remain the charming southern gentlemen society expected, but the light had gone out in his eyes.

Throughout the years he engaged in many romantic trysts, but none were worthy enough in his eyes to take Elizabeth's place in his heart or his home. That of course did not stop the ladies of New Orleans from trying their best to change his mind. There was an endless and shameless parade of women willing to do anything they could to win Peter's heart; and the title of Lady of the Manor. Peter was one of the most eligible bachelors in town; but much to the dismay of his wanton love interests, he was fond of sampling a variety of sweets, but he never sampled one irresistible enough that he could stomach having it daily.

Although John missed having a mother around to provide that nurturing touch; none of his father's long litany of bedfellows was interested in nurturing anything but their social and financial status as the new Mrs. Devereux. It didn't bother John that his father never selected a new wife, in his mind each candidate was worse than the last and would only be an insult to his mother's memory.

Thoughts of his mother brought tears to his eyes. She had been gone now for almost sixteen years and the actual anniversary of her death was right around the corner. Elizabeth had died on December 10, 1840. It was his mother that came up with the idea of having the elaborate New Year's Eve parties; and allowing the house slaves to attend as guests. It was her favorite time of year; she said it gave everyone in the world a chance to start over and do things differently.

After her death, Peter continued the annual gala in his wife's memory. John wished that she was here to comfort him now; but more than anything he yearned for his mother's words to be true. How happy he would be if the world itself took that opportunity to do things differently; and his mother could be here to embrace his family, the one he actually wanted.

John wished that society could be colorblind, and everyone could choose their own destiny. America is supposed to be the land of freedom; but if it truly was free, then, Marie could be my wife and we could celebrate the birth of our twins together! John thought. We could mark this occasion in true Devereux fashion, hosting a party for all of New Orleans to bask in our happiness, he fantasized.

Those thoughts felt comforting and warm and for a moment John became lost in them; but the cold hand of reality soon reached in and chilled him to the bone. The world wasn't a different place and even if his mother was here, she could not change the fact that Marie was a slave that could never be his wife; or the fact that he could never be the father or husband he truly wanted to be. From the outside looking in, John's life looked like heaven, but inside he was trapped in his own private hell. He faced a future of watching the woman he loved live as the wife of another man; and watching both her and their child live life as slaves.

John became overwhelmed with his circumstances and the feeling of being trapped by them. He wanted to escape this life and be free from being haunted by his grief. Clutching his now half empty bottle of whiskey, John decided to forgo the formalities of a glass. For the pain he was now feeling, he drank straight from the bottle, hoping that the dark liquid could numb his broken heart.

Cold Comfort

Winter 1856

A month had passed since the twins' unexpected arrival, so Peter felt that it was now time for the maternal switch to be made. It was December, the Christmas season, and Peter could think of no greater gift, than finally having another heir to his legacy. After all, if he expected the good people of New Orleans to believe that Helena had given birth to the child, then he couldn't let too much time pass. Although he had not been broadcasting his intentions to the world, he had made some preparations.

Dr. Sinclair was again called to the Devereux plantation to handle a delicate and top-secret task. He was to create   a birth certificate for the new heir proclaiming John as the father and Helena as the mother. Peter also took the liberty of naming the child Jonathan Devereux Jr. Since John was already on board and Helena had been instructed on how things would be, Peter need only inform Marie and Thomas. After Dr. Sinclair had left, Peter went to find Marie.

She was alone in the room nursing baby Timothy while Thomas Jr. was asleep in his bassinette. Peter opened the door and as soon as Marie looked up and met his gaze, her smile faded, and her heart dropped to the pit of her stomach. She knew the time she had been dreading since the twins were born had finally come.

"Marie, you are looking quite lovely; motherhood certainly suits you." Peter exclaimed in his charming southern drawl. But Marie knew in her heart that he was there for her baby. She knew Helena couldn't have any children and that Peter needed an heir to be born to fuse the Devereux and Marchand families. That was the whole point of John and Helena's arranged marriage. When Marie saw the look in Peter's eyes when she gave birth to Timothy, her unexpected and white complexioned son, she knew this day would come.

Sensing that Marie knew why he was there, he didn't waste time with the formalities of his intentions; he just started telling her what a blessing his offer was to her family.

"Think about it Marie, you were only expecting to have one son and you will still be able to raise the son you expected. The other was an additional blessing that you can share with John. Now you will both have an opportunity to raise and love the children you created together. I promise I will make sure that he has the best of everything and you will be right there to watch him grow up into a fine upstanding young man."

Knowing that she had no way of fighting to keep her baby, Marie tried to take comfort in knowing that at least one of her sons would be spared the life of being a slave. Now her guilt was no longer from giving her son to Peter, but that she could not give them both to be raised as heirs instead of slaves.

Marie looked down at her baby in her arms and with sorrowful eyes filled with tears she gave him a kiss, wrapped him in his little blanket and handed him to Peter. As Peter turned to exit the room with the baby, Marie exclaimed with outstretched arms, "Mommy will always love you Timothy."

Without turning around to face her, Peter stopped at the door and responded. "His name is Jonathan Devereux Jr. now; you should try to keep that in mind, so you don't make that mistake in the future."

Marie's heart broke in a million pieces as she began to sob uncontrollably. Thomas who was just coming up to check on his wife and sons saw Peter leaving with the baby. Forgetting his station in life, Thomas grabbed Peter's arm and said, "Where are you going with my son?"

Not wanting things to get worse Marie jumped to her feet and grabbed her husband. "Thomas no, just let him go!' she pleaded.

Peter turned to a grief-stricken Thomas and said, "Son I know this is going to be difficult, but you best listen to your wife before things get a whole lot worse. You wouldn't want her to lose a son and a husband all in the same day now would you?"

Realizing that he had no rights to fight for his son, Thomas released his grip on Peter's arm and let him leave with the baby. As they watched their son being taken away forever, Thomas and Marie held each other and cried. They knew they had to accept that their son was gone, but they would never forget he was theirs.

Although Peter had been spinning his immaculate tale about his new grandson's birth and Helena's top-secret pregnancy with usual flare, some were still finding the story a little hard to believe. Though none were brave enough to voice their suspicions to his face, there were plenty of quiet whispers and speculation going on behind his back. Not wanting those whispers and speculation to uncover his secret, Peter had to find a way to salvage this situation without his web of lies unraveling before his eyes.

Peter's train of thought was interrupted by a knock at the door. Soon Sarah emerged with a letter from Peter's Uncle Thaddeus. Although Sarah was not happy with her daughter's suffering, she knew her grandson would have a better life, so she focused her efforts more on comforting her daughter than punishing the Devereuxs. She gave Peter the letter and left the room. Curious as to what his Uncle could possibly want; Peter poured himself a glass of whiskey and opened the letter.

My Dear Nephew Peter,

Although our meeting didn't go quite as I'd hoped, I did accomplish my goal; I met my only surviving relative and got to meet my little brother's son. Though I wished we would have had more opportunities to get to know each other better, I am afraid that shall not be the case. If you are reading this letter now, it is because I have passed on from this life and this is to be my last will and testament.

All the documents are with my lawyer T. D. Banks, Esq. and I have enclosed his address in this letter. Sadly, I had no children of my own, so as my only heir I am leaving you my entire fortune which includes a number of slaves and a vast estate here on Tobacco Road.

I know we did not see eye to eye on a lot of things, but your strength and determination reminded me of a younger version of myself. Since my visit to your home, my health had been on a steady decline. For years I have suffered with a mysterious stomach ailment that made me wish for death; and since you are now reading this letter, it seems the good Lord finally granted that wish. No need to worry about funeral arrangements, I have had my attorney tend to my final arrangements. He will be expecting you to take over the deed and property within 30 days after receiving this letter. Smile Peter; you are now a very wealthy man. Use your fortune wisely and guard it with your life, because good fortune always has a way of bringing out the bad in people.

Sincerely,
Thaddeus J. Devereux

After reading the letter, Peter became emotional, not with sadness for Uncle Thaddeus' passing, he had no love for the man; no, his emotion was of joy. Uncle Thaddeus had just given Peter the answer to his dilemma. He would move his family and their secrets to his uncle's tobacco plantation in North Carolina. His new increased fortune will make him the wealthiest man in the Carolinas and the distance from New Orleans would ensure his secrets stayed secret.

Plans were already being made for the Devereux annual New Year's Eve gala, now it would also be a grand farewell to New Orleans as well. Uncle Thaddeus may have never been there for me or my father growing up; nor had any other redeemable qualities as a human being, but he sure came through for me in the end! Whew! Thank you, Uncle Thaddeus, Peter reflected.

As he put the letter down, Peter had the feeling he'd just been handed another unexpected blessing. My grandson will celebrate his first Christmas here at his family's original home; and we will formally introduce him to society. Then, before people can start picking and prodding about his paternity, we will bid New Orleans adieu in grand fashion at the annual gala. This New Year's will symbolize a new life for the Devereux family! Peter thought to himself.

Isn't it funny, that Marie and John conceived my unexpected little blessing at the last New Year's Eve gala; now, Uncle Thaddeus bestowed yet another blessing in time for this year's event? Elizabeth darling, you were right; this is the season for everyone to have another chance to do things differently! He smiled to himself and then hurried to inform the rest of the family; and prepare them to make the move to their new life.

The plantation was in a frenzy preparing for this grand event and for the family's departure. There was so much to do and in such a short time. There was no time to waste and no room for error. Christmas was celebrated on a small scale that year, because the focus was on the impending move.

Everyone was also getting adjusted to their new roles within the new Devereux family; which was not an easy task for anyone, especially Marie and Thomas. Not being able to really celebrate her son's first Christmas the way she had hoped was just another reminder that as a slave, nothing, including your flesh and blood belongs to you.

Although Helena had now recovered from her ordeal, she did not emerge a better person. She certainly did not develop any maternal instincts. Especially for a child that served as a constant reminder that her husband had an affair with a slave. So, Marie was still enlisted to take care of John Jr. as his nanny. Marie found some strange comfort in that, because at least then she knew she could still shower all the love she could on her son and that he would be well taken care of.

After weeks of secrecy and planning, the day had finally arrived for the Devereux's grand farewell party and introduction of baby John Jr. New Orleans was all a buzz about the event and only the crème de la crème was invited to attend. Although Winston Dubois would never have been placed on that guest list, he had no intention of missing the party. He dressed in his finest suit and managed to sneak in amongst the other party guests. He kept a low profile, as his purpose for attending was to gather information, not disrupt the festivities. Winston observed as people milled around eating hors d'oeuvres and sipping the finest champagne. It seemed that the party was for everyone else because the Devereuxs were not in attendance. Time seemed to drag on forever and then finally the hosts of the evening emerged.

John, Helena and John Jr. were all dressed in garments of matching fabrics and looked like the perfect family. However, Winston noticed that when Helena was holding her new baby she looked very awkward and uneasy, not at all like a doting new mother. He also noticed that Marie looked like she was in anguish watching the display; and when John Jr. began to cry uncontrollably, it was Marie who rushed to the infant and soothed his cries.

All these little signs gnawed at Winston, and he latched onto his suspicions like a dog on a bone. As well- wishers gathered to sneak a peek at the new bundle of joy, their curiosities were also peaked.

"Why Helena he is absolutely gorgeous; you must be so proud," an older lady in a grand hat stated, peering at the infant.

Nervously Helena replied, "Yes, I am, there is nothing I love more than being his mother".

Looking at how visibly uncomfortable and awkward Helena looked, the lady replied, "Well you would never know by how nervous and fidgety you are my dear, you look as if you never held a baby in your life; certainly not like you are holding your own baby."

The old woman's comments made Helena even more nervous and worried that someone would suspect it was not really her child. Sensing her uneasiness, John Jr. began to cry again, and Helena snapped, yelling at the infant "be quiet!" The display garnered the attention of not only the older lady, who looked appalled, but John as well.

"Don't take it out on my son because he knows you are not and never will be his mother. A jackal has more maternal instincts than you," John spat.

Helena was now completely on edge and responded frantically "How am I supposed to bond with the bastard   son of my husband and his slave whore?"

The altercation between Helena and John was starting to draw attention. Even though no one heard what they were saying, the tense body language and confrontational stance between them was hard to miss. It also didn't go unnoticed by their uninvited guest, Winston Dubois. Fearing that Helena was going to sabotage his well laid plans, Peter came over to intervene. He had worked much too hard to set his well laid plan in motion and no one was going to derail it now.

Peter approached John and Helena with a smile on his face, but daggers shooting from his eyes. "Marie, come take John Jr. up to bed, I fear all this excitement is too much for him; and his mother," Peter said, letting his last statement out through clenched teeth while staring a hole through Helena.

Breaking his glare, Helena cast her eyes to the other side of the room and gave Marie the baby. As soon as he was in Marie's arms, John Jr. quieted down, placing his little hands aside her face and cooing happily.

The Devereuxs were so fixated on maintaining their farce, that they still had not noticed Winston, soaking up every nuance of their little charade. After Marie had taken John Jr upstairs, Peter tried to redirect his guest's attention to the climax of the evening; the entrance of a new year.

"Come everyone; grab a glass of champagne to toast in the New Year!" Peter exclaimed, pointing towards the trays of full glasses circulating about the room.

Feeling that he had all he needed to confirm his suspicion, Winston slipped out of the party before the countdown unnoticed; and went home to plan his next move. He had big plans for his new year as well; getting Marie and destroying the Devereuxs. Inside, the party was in full swing as the guests excitedly counted down in unison. Once the count reached 1, bags of confetti which hung above the ballroom, were released.

Everyone toasted and smiled as they wished each other a Happy New Year. 1857 was now upon them and it was time for the party to end. Peter bid everyone a good night, stating that his family had a long journey ahead of them the next morning and needed to get some rest. Everyone left, bidding their final farewells and best wishes.

Once the last guest had left the party, Peter immediately turned his attention to Helena. With a venomous stare he warned, "I don't care if you have to take acting classes to pull this off, but you will learn how to at least appear like a good mother in public. In private, since it's obvious that you have absolutely no maternal instincts or common sense, Marie will take care of the baby."

Helena was about to open her mouth to object, but thought it better to remain silent. Exhausted from trying to keep up appearances, Peter left his son and daughter in law with final instructions. "Now go get some sleep, we all have a long day ahead of us; tomorrow we bid farewell to the prying eyes and suspicions of New Orleans and hello to a new life in North Carolina." He then left and retired to bed.

Without further words, John and Helena did the same. Marie and Thomas had also retired to their room, but rest was something that would elude them that night. 1857 may have been the beginning of a bright new future for the Devereux family, but for Marie and Thomas, it was the continuation of their same nightmare. The year and the town in which they would live may be different, but their status would still be the same. No matter the location of the plantation, they would always be slaves. Marie imagined that she was feeling only a minuscule amount of the agony her mother must have felt when she was separated from her husband and son.

Although watching her son grow up without knowing she was his mother would be painful for Marie, at least she would get to watch him grow up. Marie couldn't begin to comprehend what her mother goes through each day, not knowing if her husband and son are even still alive. Feeling that this line of thinking was only making her sadness worsen, Marie kissed her son TJ goodnight, said a prayer for John Jr and tried to sleep. The next day the Devereuxs would pack and leave New Orleans and the threat of their secret being exposed would be left behind, or so they thought.

Family is a Dirty Business

Spring 1857

Crashing the Devereux's farewell bash, proved even more helpful than Winston had hoped. He thought about how strange Helena was acting; and that she was not behaving at all like a new mother. He also noticed how pained Marie looked every time she saw the baby. Helena was supposed to be this doting mother, but when the baby started crying, it was Marie and not Helena that stepped in to console him. Winston was sure that something was off. That coupled with the fact that he knew that Marie had been pregnant, but Helena was never seen looking remotely like she was with child, made Winston's deviously inquisitive mind think something was not quite right. Maybe this move was not so much to take care of family business as it was to hide family secrets. Winston thought.

After the Devereuxs had moved to their new home, Winston became obsessed with uncovering whatever secrets Peter was trying to hide. And one night, fate would hand him a golden opportunity. Dr. Sinclair, who was the Devereux family physician, was sitting at the bar having a drink and Winston decided he would join him.

"Why Dr. Sinclair, you look as if you have something on your mind, or maybe you are hoping that whiskey you keep downing will help you forget."

Dr. Sinclair looked up and saw Winston standing there wearing an ominous grin. "What the hell do you want Dubois?" said a visibly inebriated Dr. Sinclair.

"Oh, is that anyway to talk to a man that is here to offer you a friendly hand?" Winston responded feigning offense.

In an elitist tone, Dr. Sinclair quipped, "Humph, there is nothing you have that I could ever possibly need or want! Now leave me alone you vagabond and let me drink in peace."

The doctor's snubbing was a stinging reminder to Winston that he was of the lowest class and that made him very angry. Winston sat down beside the doctor grabbing his arm as he was about to take another drink. Appalled that Winston would have the audacity to think he was privileged enough to lay his hands on him, Dr. Sinclair grabbed Winston's hand and pried it from his replying, "Have you taken leave of your senses Dubois? The drink you are spilling is worth more than you!"

Visibly angry, Winston spat between grit teeth, "You're no better than me old man; and I bet you would be very interested in what I know about you! Or better yet, the good people of New Orleans would be interested to know about your secret services you have provided for the Devereuxs."

Although Winston didn't have any concrete proof of his suspicions, he knew that Dr. Sinclair could give him all that he needed. Dr. Sinclair turned white as a sheet and replied, "What secret services?"

That trademark sinister smile returned to Winston's face and he replied, "That's what you're going to tell me, or I am going to tell your wife that you have squandered away all of her inheritance on gambling, booze and prostitutes."

Not willing to risk his wife finding out about his secret life, Dr. Sinclair confessed his sins as if he were talking to his priest; and by the time he was done, Winston had all the ammunition he needed to go after the Devereuxs. He immediately went back to his home and prepared his plan of attack. That night he was like a kid before Christmas morning excited about what Santa was going to leave under the tree, but the only gift he wanted this year was Marie and a piece of the Devereux fortune; both of which he was willing to take by force.

The next morning, Winston went into town to gather all he needed for the trip. He stopped by Dr. Sinclair's office to pick up a copy of the phony birth certificate that proclaimed Helena and John as the parents of the new Devereux heir and a signed confession from Dr. Sinclair that the birth certificate was forged.

Although he didn't want to betray Peter, Dr. Sinclair knew that if he didn't give Winston what he wanted, he was going to ruin his marriage and his practice, but he also knew that once Peter found out about his betrayal he was going to ruin his life.

Distraught over his decision and feeling he had no way out; Dr. Sinclair decided he had reached the end.

When Winston entered the Doctor's office he found the documents he sought on the desk and the doctor with his brains splattered all over the wall courtesy of his own gun. Seeing the display Winston said with a smirk, "Damn Doc, you didn't have to kill yourself, I would have gladly done it for you."

Winston noticed the safe where Dr. Sinclair kept his gun was open and had a stack of cash in it. "Guess you won't need this anymore," Winston said with a laugh and put the cash into his bag. Then he picked up the envelope and left the office as if nothing had happened.

Winston took his ill-gotten money over to the bar and had a drink while he plotted his next move. He needed to find out exactly where the Devereuxs had gone and no one around town was willing to tell him that information. All he needed was a place to start and he could go from there, fortunately for him greed was always a weakness that could be exploited.

Winston knew that the Devereuxs' attorney would know where they were headed, because he needed to know where to send his paperwork. He also knew there was no way Peter's attorney would talk to him, he didn't need Winston's money, but his law clerk did. For a very little bribe, the law clerk told Winston that the Devereuxs had moved to a tobacco plantation in North Carolina willed to Peter by his Uncle Thaddeus. The information was all Winston needed to begin his search. He prepared to leave for Tobacco Road at first light.

Meanwhile in North Carolina, the Devereuxs were settling into their new life quite nicely. They were all moved in and taking their place in North Carolina high society. But they were not the only ones who received a happy reception upon their arrival. When the Devereuxs arrived, Peter took inventory of his new slaves to figure out where the old ones would now be placed. It was discovered that Sarah's husband Nathaniel and son Jacob were among the slaves Peter had just inherited.

Nathaniel had never remarried and had raised Jacob to be a fine young man. Even though Nathaniel's darker skin would have typically put him in the fields (and did when Thaddeus was alive), Peter felt Sarah and Marie also deserved something good out of this move, so he allowed Nathaniel to move in the room with Sarah, and Jacob to move into the house as well.

Peter's soft heart wasn't the only reason for the decision. He was no fool; though he had no proof, he knew Sarah was not someone he wanted as an enemy, and given what her daughter had recently been put through, he thought this was a way to get on her and Marie's good side again.

Marie was so happy to finally meet her father and her older brother. She had dreamed of their faces and what they were like almost every night, but nothing could compare to the feeling she felt when she actually came face to face with her family. Nathaniel was so happy to find that not only did he get his wife and daughter back, but he had a brand-new son in law and grandson as well. Sarah thought it best to save the story of their other grandchild to a later date; for now, she just wanted to enjoy her happiness.

Sarah had gone by her maiden name Jean-Baptiste and had her daughter go by it as well when she and her husband were separated. She never thought she would see them again and, so she forced her mind to pretend her husband and son never existed. She did tell Marie about them and why they were not with them, but she rarely discussed them at length; the memories were too painful. Now that they were together again, Sarah would wear her married name of Monet, with extreme pride.

When Sarah was reunited with her husband and her son, there was a light in her eyes that Peter had never seen before; but he recognized it very well. It was the light he used to see in his wife Elizabeth's eyes when she would see him enter the room; and the smile on Nathaniel's face reminded Peter of his own. In that moment, he saw that slave or master, true love is unmistakable and irreplaceable.

Although Peter was not searching for a replacement for his true love, it didn't take the women of North Carolina long to start lining up to see who could land the newest and richest bachelor in town. Watching the endless and shameless parade of women who did everything from bake enough food to fill up a bakery, to dressing as provocative as the law (and southern values) would allow, gave the whole family, including the slaves, a good laugh.

Each time a new potential bride showed up trying to use her cooking skills, good breeding, or ability to fill out a custom-made dress to catch Peter's eye; everyone knew they were in for a treat. As soon as their carriage would stop in front of the house, the family and the slaves would all run to see what show was playing today; and they never disappointed. Some of them even tried to win favor by entertaining Peter. The Devereux household had so many pianists, violinists, and vocalists coming through the door they thought they were living in a concert hall.

Peter politely endured the various performances and thoroughly enjoyed their more carnal efforts to advance their status. The various baked goods and casseroles he usually gave to the slaves to enjoy, and even they threw some of them away. There seemed to be a more jovial spirit in the air and everyone could feel it. It seemed to make people all over the plantation a little bit nicer.

Maybe it was the country air or the expansion of his fortune, but Peter was breathing a lot easier on Tobacco Road. Marie was happier because she was still able to take care of her son, but sad that he could never know that she was his mother. Helena was softening to the role of mother and even asked Marie for some help on learning how to take care of him. Given the circumstances things were as good as they could be.

Peter was just getting into the groove of how things worked in North Carolina and making friends with the right people. Neither of which was hard to do given his last name and enormous fortune. He joined all the appropriate social clubs and committees and attended every socialite event that happened in the area.

Peter had positioned himself right where he needed to be in high society and his home life was one of peace. Given that he was nowhere close to being the cantankerous tyrant that his uncle was, the slaves thought they had died and gone to heaven; so there wasn't any uproar on the plantation.

Not being a cruel man by nature, Peter didn't believe in beating and killing his slaves to keep them in line (though he wouldn't think twice about killing anyone who threatened him or his family). He also didn't believe in mistreating and humiliating them. If times were different he wouldn't own slaves at all and had thought at one time about freeing them.

Peter changed his mind when he started hearing the stories of free men and women being beaten and lynched. He knew at least he could protect the ones he had from anyone else doing anything to them.

Although the business of slavery left a bitter taste in his mouth, he did profit from it substantially; and he didn't mind sharing the wealth. Peter was a businessman and he knew the two most important rules of business: rule number one, employees are the heart of every business and happy employees are more productive employees. Rule number two, you have to spend money to make money.

Peter followed those rules to the letter; and when he took over his uncle's plantation, he spent some of his enormous new fortune renovating the slave quarters. Each was now like mini cabins with wood floors to maximize warmth in the winter. Although they were still not as cozy as the main house, it was like a luxury hotel compared to what they were used to from Thaddeus.

Peter also made sure that all of his slaves had shoes   and clothing to wear; and unlike most slave masters he didn't prevent his slaves from receiving an education. He ran his plantation like a real business and his efforts proved successful. Slaves worked regular hours, and no one worked on Sunday (these were rules that his wife put in place when she was alive, and Peter continued to abide by them).

Elizabeth detested slavery and everything about it, but she was also aware of the times; so, she made Peter agree that if they had to have slaves those were the rules. Those rules had served Peter and his bank account well throughout the years; so unorthodox or not, he saw no need to change them. Peter was beginning to relax and being that his plantation was not close to anyone else's for miles, it was like they were in their own little world untouched by the outside. Little did he know that world was about to be threatened by a familiar foe; one that was vicious, obsessed and hell bent on revenge.

When Winston Dubois arrived in North Carolina, he started inquiring about the location of Peter's Plantation. He told people he was an old friend from New Orleans that came in town on business and wanted to say hello. Southern hospitality being what it was it didn't take long for

Winston to pinpoint Peter's location.

The trip from New Orleans to North Carolina was long and tiring, so Winston was exhausted. He decided to get a room; and grab something to eat and drink before heading to bed. Though he was looking forward to confronting Peter, he knew he needed his wits about him; so, he had best rest up and check out his surroundings first. Tomorrow he would go into town to find out all he could about the Devereux's new life here. He needed to know just how much Peter had to lose; so, he would know just how much to take him for.

Take my Secrets to the Grave

As the warm North Carolina sun beat down on Peter Devereux's back, he decided he would retire to his porch to admire his massive rose garden instead of taking his intended stroll through it. After he summoned one of his many house slaves to bring him a glass of lemonade, he relaxed in his favorite chair and stared out at the horizon. The combination of the sun's warmth and feeling of spring's cool breeze wafting through the air, made the experience almost euphoric.

As Peter rocked rhythmically back and forth in his rocking chair, he reflected on how blessed he was and how thankful that he was able to start over in a place where no one knew his family's secret. Staring out at his enormous new property, something slowly appeared in the distance. Peter thought he was seeing a mirage when the blurred figure of a man appeared in his view.

As the figure continued down the willow tree lined road leading to the main house, the face of Winston Dubois came into view. Suddenly, Peter's feelings of comfort were replaced with anxiety. He never thought he would see Winston again when he left New Orleans; and the hairs that were now standing up on the back of Peter's neck indicated that this was not a friendly or accidental visit.

"Evening Pete; been a long time." Winston said as he reached the first step of the porch.

"Not long enough for me," Peter replied with stoic expression.

A sinister smile crept over Winston's face. "So much for southern hospitality; now is that any way to treat an old friend? You didn't even offer me a drink." Winston replied, feigning offense.

"We're not friends and you're a long way from New Orleans; so why don't we cut to the meat of why you're here," Peter retorted. He was now standing on the edge of his porch staring down at his unwelcome visitor.

Never losing his smile, Winston put his hands in the air in mock surrender. "Not much for small talk I see. Okay, well let's get to it then. I have been asking some of these good Christian folk 'round here 'bout you and your family and it seems that you're the pinnacle of respectability. Everyone seems to think you have the perfect family; and you're the envy of all your neighbors. Now I wonder how your high society North Carolina friends would feel to know you were perpetrating a fraud," Winston said with contrived concern.

Peter descended the steps until he was standing eye to eye with Winston. "I don't know what you're implying or what the hell you think you know about me, but I'm exactly who I say I am; and I have nothing to hide." Peter replied.

"Oh, so the good White Christian folks of North Carolina know who the real mother is of the newest Devereux heir?" Winston said, never flinching.

Grabbing Winston and pushing him further away from the house, Peter quizzed, "What the hell do you want Winston? 'Cause you're treading on very dangerous ground."

Snatching away from Peter's grasp, Winston replied nonchalantly, "Well, seeing as how you are doing so well here on Tobacco Road, I thought you should share the wealth; say $250,000 and Marie to start."

Peter's jaw tightened and through clinched teeth he quizzed, "And if I don't?"

The sinister smile slowly returned to Winston's face as he responded, "Well then it will be my civic duty to inform all your high society friends that your grandson is really a nigger. I wonder how many social invites your family will get then."

Staring at Winston standing there being so smug about destroying everything he had worked so hard to build made something inside of Peter snap and his eyes grew cold as he replied, "Ok Winston; I don't have that kind of money just lying around, so it will take some time for me to get it."

Gloating in his supposed victory, Winston spat, "You have until the end of the week to get me my money, or everyone in town is gonna know about your nigger grandson!"

Peter coolly replied. "If $250,000 will shut you up and get you out of our lives, I will be more than happy to give it to you. I'll even make sure that Marie is prepared to go with her new Master. Meet me down by the lake at the edge of my property Friday at midnight. I will make sure that I have your money and Marie waiting for you."

Feeling like he had finally gotten the best of Peter, Winston agreed. "Alright; midnight it is. You better have my money, or I will make sure everyone knows your dirty little secret."

With a dark look in his eyes, Peter replied, "Oh don't worry Winston, I will make sure that you'll get exactly what you have coming to you." As Winston turned to leave, Peter started making plans on how he was going to shut Winston up for good.

All that evening Peter was in his own world thinking of ways to get rid of Winston. As much as he would like to see the look on his smug face when he put a bullet right between his eyes, he knew he would have a hard time explaining that to the police. No, he had to be very careful with how he was going to dispose of his uninvited guest.

Peter had worked very hard to cover up his family's secret and build a new life here on Tobacco Road; and the only thing worse than having Winston there causing trouble, would be having Winston's death causing the police to snoop around in his family's past affairs. The thought made Peter want to kill Winston even more.

Peter was in the library fuming about his interaction with Winston. "That vagrant is becoming more trouble than he is worth! At first, he was a minor irritation that was not worth my attention; but now he's becoming a real nuisance and he has to be dealt with. Oh! If you wanted my attention Winston, you most certainly have it now. I am going to focus all my attention on getting rid of you for good! No one threatens my family, no one! And Marie may be a slave, but I would never turn her over to the likes of you, you degenerate monster!" He said aloud shaking his closed fists together as if they were around Winston's neck.

Peter was so enthralled that he didn't notice that Sarah was standing in the doorway watching and listening to the whole display. She knew what would happen to Marie if Winston succeeded in his plan and she was more than willing to help Peter with Winston's demise.

"Having some troubles Master Devereux?" Sarah said breaking Peter's tirade.

"Nothing for you to be concerned about Sarah; I apologize if I was disturbing the house, I thought I was alone," Peter said, regaining his composure.

" Seems the one that's disturbed is you sir, can I help in any way?" Sarah offered.

"Thanks, but no, my troubles are unfortunately beyond your assistance," Peter replied, rubbing his forehead to calm the growing headache he was feeling.

"Don't be so sure. Not to overstep, but I couldn't help but overhear that Mr. Dubois was in town causing some troubles for you," Sarah said, leading Peter to reveal his need to rid the world of Winston.

"You overheard that huh? Well unfortunately the only way to rid us all of Winston is to kill him, and regrettably, murder is still illegal," Peter said, taking a sip of his whiskey.

"Not if they cannot prove it was murder. Accidents and unexplained illnesses happen all the time," Sarah said, no longer being obscure.

The hairs on the back of Peter's neck stood on end as he processed Sarah's ominous words. Being desperate to eliminate Winston without serving a jail sentence, Peter was open to anything. He listened while Sarah told him how she could help him get rid of Winston without it ever being traced to him or even considered a homicide.

Peter was intrigued and a little frightened that Sarah seemed so confident in her ability to help disguise Winston's demise as an accident, but he had to admit he had no other options. "Not that I am not appreciative of your wanting to help me with this problem, but why are you helping me?" Peter asked.

"Because Mr. Dubois threatened my family as well; he wants my daughter and I will die before I let him take her," Sarah replied with eyes so dark they made Peter's blood run cold. He knew Sarah had a vested interest in seeing Winston disappear forever as well, so he trusted her with his plan; and she told him what they needed to do to carry it out.

"Get an old sack and stuff it with newspaper and bring it to me. When Mr. Dubois comes to meet you I'll be hiding in the bushes with the sack for you to give to him," Sarah said.

"So, I'm going to give him the money? That's your plan?" Peter asked.

"No, the sack will contain newspaper and an added surprise, but you will not have to give him one red cent," Sarah assured.

Looking confused, Peter asked, "Isn't he going to know something is wrong when he opens the bag and he sees that nothing's in there but newspaper?"

A smile appeared on Sarah's face as she said, "Trust me Master Devereux, when Mr. Dubois opens that sack he will not be worried about the fact that no money is inside, and we will not have to worry about Mr. Dubois ever again!"

Peter was curious about what Sarah was going to do, but he trusted her and didn't ask anything further. He just went to gather the sack and newspaper as he was instructed. All week Winston was spending money around town like water, celebrating his impending new fortune and new concubine Marie. He had dreamed of what he would do to her ever since the first day he saw her. His obsession with her was terrifying to more than just Marie. Winston's appetite for sadistic torture and rape was legendary and another reason he was shunned by those upstanding citizens of New Orleans.

Although Winston was not poor, he was still a man of meager means by their standards; soon Peter Devereux was about to help him change all of that, or so he thought. He was giddy at the thought of bringing Peter Devereux to his knees. He was almost as excited about that as he was acting out his carnal pleasures with Marie; almost. Winston began looking around the town for any available property. He was about to come into a substantial amount of money and he deserved a home that would showcase his good fortune. He felt that it was time for him to relocate and start anew; and he thought what better place to do that than right here.

Humph! The Devereuxs seem to have been able to reinvent themselves in North Carolina; maybe here I can do the same. I will move everything here and start over; and I won't have to deal with the snobbish people in New Orleans looking down their pointy noses at me. I can be a man of status and considerable means. Maybe even get invited to some of those high-class parties with pretty socialites competing to dance with me. Winston laughed to himself as he pretended to accept an offer to dance and spun his imaginary partner around the room.

When his dance was complete, he fell on the bed and placed his hands behind his head; staring up at the ceiling with a smile on his face, Winston thought he was finally going to get his just due. The thought of staying in North Carolina and rubbing his new fortune in Peter's face was a bonus.

Back on Tobacco Road, Peter was now feeling strangely at ease. It was hard to explain, but ever since he confided in Sarah, his tension eased. It was as if he knew that now everything was going to be okay. Although Sarah had not given him the details on exactly how the plan was going to work, he had complete confidence in her. He knew that she was not going to take a chance on Winston getting his hands on her daughter, especially not since she had finally gotten her family back.

The week had crept by slowly, but soon Friday had arrived, and it was time to set the plan into action. Peter and Sarah spent that day milling about the plantation doing their normal routines, but both were clear about the time they were to meet Winston for their final encounter. Peter had found an old cloth sack and filled it with shreds of newspaper and gave it to Sarah as she had instructed. Peter didn't see the sack again until it was time to meet Winston that night, so he had no idea how a sack full of Newspaper was supposed to rid them of their nemesis.

At 11:45pm, Peter made his way down to the lake at the edge of his property. The night held an unusual coolness for that time of year, and everything was eerily quiet. Peter thought the atmosphere was strangely appropriate for the task they were about to perform.

When he arrived, Sarah was already there with the cloth sack in hand. She handed it to Peter and instructed him not to open it or even pick it up until he handed it to Winston. Peter nodded that he understood and did as instructed. He stood beside the sack being careful not to move it until Winston arrived. Sarah went to hide in the woods and watch. Fifteen minutes passed before Winston arrived visibly intoxicated. He stumbled over to where he saw Peter standing and mockingly tipped his hat.

"Hello Pete; how are you this fine evening?" Winston slurred.

"Annoyed; you're late," Peter responded.

Laughing, Winston said, "Oh I'm sorry Pete, I

didn't mean to keep you waiting; I know how you hoity toity types like punctuality."

Peter was looking at Winston and imagining the smile melting from his face when he met with whatever ill fate Sarah had planned for him.

"Let's get this over with Dubois, so I can be rid of you. I have your money right here." Peter said, lifting the sack to give it to Winston.

"Hold on just one minute there; something or should I say someone is missing. I don't see the lovely Marie anywhere. You know she is a very important part of this deal Pete. Without her, your money means nothing to buy my silence," Winston said, barely able to stand up.

"She'll be down in a second. I thought you might like a moment alone with your money first, while her mother gets her nice and pretty for you," Peter said, staring at Winston with a smile.

"Woo hoo! Now that's what I'm talking about Pete, I'm glad that you finally came to your senses and stopped trying to fight me on this. When I make up my mind about something, you can bet I'm gonna do whatever I have to do to get it" Winston replied.

Peter gritted his teeth as Winston continued, "That's the difference between you and me Pete; you stand behind your morals and codes of being a southern gentleman. Well the only code I stand behind is getting what I want no matter who I have to destroy to get it; and what I want is Marie. I've been dreaming about what I am going to do that pretty little piece of chocolate. Who knows Pete, maybe she can sire some of my offspring too. Hell, if it's good enough for the Devereuxs its good enough for the Dubois!" Winston laughed as he took the sack from Peter's hands.

Not sure what was going to happen next, Peter stood back after handing the bag to Winston and peered over his shoulder to see if he could spot Sarah hiding in the woods. He was looking for some sign of what he should do. Seeing no glimpse of Sarah, Peter turned his attention back to Winston. He didn't want him to see him looking around and get suspicious.

"Don't you want to count it first?" Peter asked, anxious for Winston to open the sack.

Winston paused, then pointing at Peter he replied with a laugh, "Humph! You're right Pete; I wouldn't want you to try to pull a fast one! I know how you Devereuxs hate to lose; especially to the likes of me. Guess you're gonna have to get used to it now ain't ya? 'Cause this time, someone from 'the lower class' has brought the mighty Peter Devereux to his knees!" Winston laughed so hard to himself, he almost dropped the bag.

"Whoa, I better be careful, I wouldn't want to lose all your hard-earned money," Winston said, still laughing.

Peter watched in nervous anticipation, as Winston opened the sack and reached inside. At first it appeared that nothing was going to happen, when all of a sudden Peter saw Winston's smile of delight turn into a look of pure terror. When Winston removed his arm, three copper head snakes began leaping out of the sack and leveraging venomous bites all over his face and body. He tried to fight them off, but it was too late. The snakes had already begun exacting their very own brand of justice.

Winston screamed in agony as the snakes continued to attack. The venom was now coursing through his veins and shutting down his organs. He writhed in pain as he fought for his very breath. Winston stumbled backwards and landed in the lake. The snakes still attached to his body, as they escorted him to hell. Sarah emerged from the woods and stood beside Peter. Neither of them spoke a word as they watched a stunned Winston sink to his watery grave.

Out of Sight, Out of Mind

Summer 1857

After they sent Winston to his new home beneath the lake, Peter and Sarah shared one look that signaled 'it's over now'; and they never spoke of the incident again. They both walked calmly back to the house and went to their respective rooms and went to sleep. Although murdering a man would typically keep anyone that wasn't a sociopath awake at night; knowing that a monster like Winston Dubois would never be able to hurt anyone else again, made both Sarah and Peter sleep better than either could remember sleeping before.

The next morning, Sarah woke with a smile that was as bright as the morning sun. She dressed and went downstairs to get breakfast started and tend to her morning housework. As she worked she did something that she had not done in years, she started singing. Sarah had a beautiful voice, but when her husband and son were sold away, she didn't feel she had anything to sing about.

But God had not only sent her husband and son back to her safely, they were no longer living under the threat of a dangerous enemy. For the first time in a long time, Sarah had a reason to sing. Sarah's melodious voice and the sweet-smelling aromas of the breakfast she was making worked better than an alarm clock to rouse the rest of the house. One by one, members of the Devereux clan arrived in the kitchen to see what was going on.

There was something different in the air that morning and it wasn't just the sound of Sarah's beautiful voice or the smells from her good cooking; it was something else. No one could put their finger on it, but the sun seemed to shine brighter, the birds seemed to chirp louder; and all signs pointed to it being a good day.

"Morning Sarah; I tell you it is one beautiful day! I don't think I have slept that good in years. Now to wake to the smells of your good cooking and my families' bright shining faces, it's more than any man could ask for." Peter proclaimed with a huge grin.

"Why yes, it is a beautiful day indeed Master Devereux; and I predict this is only the beginning." Sarah responded with a smile that equally matched Peter's.

Peter and Sarah continued with their cheery attitudes, despite their families' perplexed look. Finally, John spoke aloud what was on everyone else's mind. "Have you two been drinking whiskey for breakfast? Ya'll both buzzing around here like two deranged honey bees."

Looking at his son's confused expression, Peter burst into laughter. "Son, I realize that this family hasn't always had a lot to smile about, but that is about to change. We are truly blessed son. We have an enormous fortune, we are all in good health and it's about time we started counting those blessings. Now let's stop questioning that happiness and enjoy this wonderful breakfast Sarah's prepared."

Sarah prepared plates of food for the Devereuxs and served them in the dining room; then she served her own family in the kitchen. As Sarah set down to join her family for breakfast, they were equally as inquisitive as to why she was in an elated mood.

"Mama is you alright? I ain't ever seen you this happy before," Marie asked, looking at her mother.

"Yeah hummingbird, you acting mighty spry dis mo'nin," Nathaniel stated, using the nickname he gave her when they met.

Even Sarah's face looked different, younger; and although everyone was happy to see this new Sarah, they still wondered what happened to bring her out. Sarah lovingly put her hands on the side of her husband's face and said, "I just woke up this morning and it hit me, how blessed I was to have my family back and I made up my mind I was going to start enjoying that happiness."

Smiling back at his wife, Nathaniel said, "Mmm hmm, so you an Masta Devereux must've tended da same revival las night 'cause ya bof flittin 'round heh like ya had sum of dat cone licka."

Everyone at the table laughed, and Sarah just gave her husband a kiss and said, "From now on, I'm going to be drunk on happiness. Now stop asking all these questions and let's eat 'fore the food gets cold. We have a lot to do today."

Although they were all still curious, they resigned to just revel in happiness for a while, because no one knew how long it would last. The days moved on and it was like a magic spell was over the plantation. For the first time anyone could ever remember, everything was calm and at peace.

Even the Devereux family took a moratorium on fighting amongst themselves and focused on enjoying life. Marie and Thomas grew closer by the day as they raised their son, and although John still hated Helena, he loved his son and spent all the time he could with him. This made it easier on Marie; to know that at least her son would grow up with one of his true parents and that he would never know the life of a slave. And since Helena was still not that maternal, Marie practically raised her other son as well.

Marie performed all the motherly duties for her other son, he just didn't know she was his mother; and that sometimes broke Marie's heart. But knowing that it could always be much worse than what it was and that she still got to see him grow up, gave her comfort. Every day she was amazed at how much her sons were growing and how close they were becoming. There on Tobacco Road, Marie felt she was finally home.

Weeks rolled by and there was not one word about Winston's disappearance. For the first week, Peter would sometimes have little twinges of anxiety that Winston's body would wash up on his property, or the police would somehow link his murder to him, but after nothing happened, Peter put those thoughts out of his mind. He rationalized that Winston was a horrible man and that no one would even miss him, let alone look for him. Those thoughts assuaged his anxiety and replaced it with a sense of confidence that Winston took his secret to the grave and in the grave, is where it would stay.

Peter and Sarah had almost forgotten about that night and Winston, like it was all just a bad dream. Unfortunately, that bad dream was about to come back to haunt them. The day started off like any other, but somehow it was different. Sarah felt it in the pit of her stomach. Something or someone was coming; and they were bringing trouble. She couldn't put her finger on what it was, and she didn't know what or who was the cause for this feeling; but she knew whatever it was, it was not good.

In a true déjà vu moment, Peter was again sitting on his porch looking out at the horizon, when he saw an image that almost made his heart stop. In the distance he saw the image of a man; and the closer the man got, the more he looked just like a younger version of Winston Dubois. Peter was frozen as his mind started racing. It couldn't be Winston, I watched Winston die in front of me and sink to the bottom of the lake. Peter thought as he dropped his glass of water and shards of glass and watery liquid spilled everywhere.

As the Winston look alike ascended the steps he looked at Peter's astonished face and said, "You okay, Mister? You look like you seen a ghost."

Trying to regain his composure, Peter managed to say, "I'm fine; you just look like someone I used to know. What can I do for you?"

The stranger replied with a confused look. "Used to know? You no longer know this person?"

Starting to feel more and more uncomfortable with this stranger and his reason for being there, Peter repeated, "Is there something I can help you with Mr. ….?"

"Dubois, Franklin Dubois" he replied.

Peter felt like his heart stopped, but he was careful not to show it. "What can I do for you Mr. Dubois?" he asked.

Searching Peter's face for a reaction to his last name, Franklin said, "Are you Peter Devereux?"

With a steady gaze Peter replied, "Yes, I am; now what can I do for you?"

Franklin stepped onto the porch and looked Peter in the eye. "Well Mr. Devereux, my Uncle Winston wrote me a month ago and asked me to come to his plantation and look after things while he was away. He said he was coming to North Carolina to see you and would be back in no more than a week; but that was more than a month ago and he has still not come back."

With stoic expression Peter inquired, "Son, what does that have to do with me?"

Not breaking eye contact, Franklin retorted "Well I should say it has a lot to do with you, seeing as how you were the last person to see him."

Sensing that Franklin was just fishing for some information and didn't really have any proof, Peter relaxed and started trying to figure out just what

Franklin wanted from him.

"I'm not sure what conversation you had with your uncle, or where he may be, but I have not seen him. We weren't exactly friends so, I am not sure why he would tell you that he was coming to pay me a visit," Peter said.

A sly smile formed on Franklin's lips and he replied, "I never said you were friends. No, my uncle told me all about you and how you looked at him like the dirt on the bottom of your boots. But he also told me that he knew a secret about your family that was going to change all that."

Coolly Peter replied, "Oh really? What secret would
that be?"

"He didn't say in the letter, but I am guessing it had to be big for him to come all the way to North Carolina to confront you," Franklin replied.

Now that Peter was sure that Franklin didn't have any idea of what Winston had on him, or any proof that he had even seen him; he had no reason to continue to entertain him.

"Mr. Dubois, I'm not sure where your uncle is at the moment, but he is not here, and he hasn't been here. Maybe he changed his mind about coming to North Carolina all together considering there was no secret to tell." Peter sarcastically replied.

"Ah now that's where you're wrong. See I checked around town to see if my uncle was here and the lady at the inn where he was staying said he checked in three weeks ago, and then disappeared," Franklin responded, not being swayed.

Hmm, that's odd. Maybe he met some pretty young woman and decided to move on," Peter said.

"He wouldn't just disappear without a trace; and he wouldn't leave all his belongings in an inn with no word. I know something ain't right here Mister and I am going to be here in town until I find out what it is. I already alerted the police that my uncle is missing, so they are looking in to it. I am going to be here poking around too, so you're going to get to know my face really well. Have a good day now; I'll see you soon," Franklin replied. Then turned and walked away.

Peter's jaw tightened as he thought, Great! Kill one Dubois and another spring up in his place just like a damned weed!

Peter walked into the house and summoned Sarah to come to the garden. Sarah could tell by the look on Peter's face that the sinking feeling she had been feeling all day was for a reason. "Is something wrong Master Devereux?" Sarah asked, as she entered the garden to find a visibly shaken Peter staring off into space.

Peter turned towards her and replied, "I just had a visit from Franklin Dubois, Winston's nephew. He said he was in town looking into the disappearance of his uncle; and that he had the police looking into it!"

Trying to calm Peter down, Sarah replied, "Don't let that worry you Master Devereux, he has nothing but his suspicions; he has no proof. Winston's body has not even been discovered yet; and even if it is, he was killed by snake bites, we never touched him."

Sarah seemed to ease Peter's fears for the moment and he began to calm down. He trusted Sarah and knew that she was right. They hadn't touched Winston, so technically they didn't kill him, and no one could prove otherwise. Peter tried to slip back into his regular routines, but everywhere he turned in town he ran into Franklin. *He's as much of a nuisance as his uncle; maybe he needs to join him,* Peter thought. Shaking all those ideas out of his head, Peter just continued about his business as if Franklin didn't exist. He figured sooner or later that he would give up and move on.

Just when it seemed as if Franklin's visit was coming to a close, a new discovery extended his stay. After pestering the police for over a month, Winston's whereabouts were finally discovered. His bloated body floated to the surface. It had been lodged between some rocks below the surface all this time, but became dislodged as the body swelled. With the body of his uncle being discovered on Peter's property, Franklin was adamant about the police pressing charges and getting justice for his uncle's death. Not being able to ignore the evidence, the police came to question Peter about their discovery.

There was a knock at the door late that evening and Sarah entered Peter's study accompanied by Sheriff Gordon and Franklin Dubois.

"Master Devereux, these gentlemen would like to speak with you," Sarah said, ushering the men into the room.

Peter rose from his chair and greeted his unexpected guests.

"Well good evening Sheriff Gordon, what seems to be the problem?" he said.

"Sorry for disturbing you Mr. Devereux, but I need to ask you some questions. Is now a good time?" Sheriff Gordon asked.

"Sure, have a seat. Sarah will bring us some tea and a few slices of her delicious apple pie," Peter replied.

Visibly upset at how the interrogation was going, Franklin snapped, "What is this? Are we here to question a murder suspect or have a damn tea party?"

Never breaking a sweat, Peter replied, "Murder suspect? Oh my, that doesn't sound good at all. Who was murdered?"

Jumping to his feet Franklin yelled, "My uncle was murdered; and you're the one who did it, you self-righteous, son of a bitch!"

Feigning offense, Peter replied, "Winston's dead? I am so sorry for your loss son, but I had nothing to do with it. I didn't even know he was in town."

Not buying his declaration of innocence, Franklin yelled, "You're a liar! He was found on your property, floating in the lake like a goddamn blow fish!"

Peter fought to hold in his laugh at Franklin's description, and said, "I'm just as shocked as you are to learn that Winston was on my property, but I assure you that I had nothing to do with his demise."

"Like hell you didn't and when the doc finishes examining his body they are gonna come and lock you up like the animal you are!" Franklin retorted.

Sensing that this visit was going to get out of hand, Sheriff Gordon said, "Okay now, let's all just settle down. Mr. Dubois, we need to hear back from the doc about what actually happened to your uncle before we go accusing anyone of anything."

Just then, Sarah entered with a tray carrying three cups of tea and three slices of pie.

"Oh good, the pie is here. Mr. Dubois, you simply must try Sarah's cooking. It's to die for," Peter said with a sly grin.

Fuming, Franklin responded "You and that pie can go straight to hell!"

With a faked confused look, Peter said, "So is that a no on the pie?"

Intervening, Sheriff Gordon replied, "You know Mr. Devereux, I think we are just going to get on outta here. Thank you for your time; and I will be in touch when the doc finishes examining the body."

Shaking the sheriff 's hand, Peter replied, "No problem Sheriff Gordon, I do hope you find out what happened to old Winston, so his young nephew here can find some peace. Sarah, would you show these fine gentlemen out please?"

Franklin looked as if he could kill Peter with his bare hands as he exited the room with the Sheriff. Once they were a safe distance down the driveway, Sarah closed the door and returned to the room with Peter.

Noticing the look on his face Sarah reassured him again. "Go on to bed now, Master Devereux, this will all be over soon; and I promise nothing will be able to be traced back to you."

Agreeing with Sarah, Peter nodded and headed up to bed; it had been more than a long night.

Chapter Twelve

Keep Your Friends Close and Your Enemies Closer

Having Franklin Dubois in town poking around was becoming a real problem for Peter. He knew the implication alone that he had anything to do with someone's murder could cause irrevocable damage to his reputation. He moved his family to North Carolina to escape the inquisitive minds of New Orleans' high society questioning his grandson's parentage; and he was finally building the life he wanted in a place where no one knew about his secrets. But as Peter was quickly learning, sometimes you can't outrun your secrets, at least not for long.

Peter was alone in his study deep in thought about how he was going to deal with, yet another Dubois obsessed with his family. *Damn you, Winston! You are just as much of a nuisance dead as you were alive! You just couldn't leave well enough, alone could you? Couldn't accept defeat with honor like a true southern gentleman; of course, there was nothing honorable, true or gentlemanly about you to start with, so I guess this should be no surprise.*

I thought when I watched you sink to your death at the bottom of the lake I was finally rid of you; but even in death you still found a way to be a thorn in my side! And if your bloated carcass floating to the surface on my property wasn't enough, now your degenerate nephew comes to town to further complicate my life. If I didn't think his disappearance would raise suspicion, I would arrange a nice reunion in hell for the both of you! Peter thought, while gripping his monogrammed letter opener.

Helena entered the room and noticed her father-in-law now stabbing the desk with the letter opener he was gripping.

"Well, I would hate to be that desk at the moment," Helena said, smiling.

This snapped Peter out of his train of thought. With a sly grin, Peter replied, "My dear you would be an excellent substitute; now, what do you want?"

With her smile replaced by a look of fear, Helena stammered, "John Jr's first birthday will be here in a few months; and I wanted to throw him a huge party. Since his birthday is so close to Halloween, I thought it might be fun to throw him a Halloween themed party for his birthday. I know it will take a while to get everything together for the type of event I want to do, so I wanted to know what you thought about it now, so I can start planning." Helena tried to gauge her father-in-law's reaction before she said anything else.

Being preoccupied with what to do about the latest Dubois debacle, Peter had completely forgotten that his grandson's first birthday was fast approaching. It was already August and Peter had spent his summer dealing with one Dubois after the other.

"It sounds fine Helena, why don't you put something together and we'll talk about it later; I have some pressing business matters I need to attend to." Peter said looking down at some papers on his desk, hoping Helena would go away.

"Is everything alright Father Devereux? We are not having any financial problems, are we?" Helena quizzed for purely selfish reasons, in her mind money problems were the only things worth fretting over; that and John's hatred of her.

Now becoming annoyed with her presence, Peter looked up from his papers and said, "Careful darling, don't get too comfortable. You don't want to find yourself on my bad side."

Sensing that she may have overstepped, Helena quickly excused herself and left the room. Elsewhere, Marie and Thomas were excited about the twins' first birthday as well.

"Can you believe it Thomas? Our sons are gonna be one year old in a few months! This year has gone by so fast, I can hardly believe it!" Marie exclaimed with sheer excitement.

Then in an instant, sadness washed over her like a flood as she reflected on everything that happened that past year. Recognizing the cause of his wife's sudden mood change, he walked up behind her and held her in a comforting embrace.

"It's gonna be alright Marie. We have to be thankful that at least the good Lord didn't take him from us all together. We still get to love him and help raise him up. I know it's not the same as we get to do with TJ, but it could always be worse. Think of what your mother went through not being able to even see Jacob grow up; at least you didn't have to suffer that. Now your family has been reunited and we are gonna be alright. I love you Marie; and I'm here for you for whatever you need".

Thomas's gentle spirit and genuine love for her and her children warmed Marie's heart and endeared him to her. She saw her husband for the first time as just that, her husband; and partner in this life. Marie turned around and for the first time, she kissed her husband like he was the love of her life.

After almost a year of waiting, Marie finally made love to Thomas; and it was an experience that surpassed either's expectations. Although she had not let go of her love for John, she had let go of any hope they could ever be together. That act is what opened the door for Marie to discover a new world of love with Thomas.

While Marie was now consummating her union with Thomas, John still refused to sleep with Helena; choosing instead to act out his carnal pleasures with various ladies around town. Because extramarital affairs were expected from men of status, no one looked upon his actions as deplorable; and as long as it didn't become a problem that would bring disgrace to the Devereux name, his father was not concerned either. The only one who was bothered by John's infidelity was Helena, but she had learned a long time ago that her protests fell on deaf ears.

The twins' pending birthday was also on the mind of their father. John felt similar to Marie; he was excited for his sons' milestone, but sad that only one would know him as their father. He tried to avoid thinking of it and instead went to talk to Peter. John had seen Sheriff Gordon and an unknown stranger leaving the house the other night as he was returning home from a tryst with one of his conquests. He had been meaning to ask Peter about it and today he was going to.

John found Peter outside taking a stroll through his garden. "Mind if I join you?" John said, catching up to his father.

"Of course not, I always enjoy spending time with my son. Helena told me about her plans to have a Halloween themed party for John Jr. and I think it's an excellent idea," Peter said, assuming that was what his son wanted to talk about.

"So, do I father, but that's not what I wanted to talk to you about." John said.

"Oh? Then what's on your mind son?" Peter asked, stopping to look his son in the eye.

"It's about the other night. I saw Sheriff Gordon and some strange man leaving the house. Is there a problem? Are we in some kind of trouble?" John asked.

"Oh no son, everything is alright; nothing to worry about." Peter lied.

Not believing his father's story, John continued to probe. Feeling that it best that he tells John what was going on, Peter filled him in on all the details; including Winston's death and his part in it.

"Sarah's right father. If Winston died of snake bites then there shouldn't be anything that ties his death to you. His nephew is just trying to find something he can link you to, but he won't; and when he doesn't he will have no choice but to return to New Orleans and leave us alone," John said, trying to reassure his father.

"Let's hope you are right son; this is the last thing we need," Peter replied.

"Now that I know what's going on, I 'm going to keep a close eye on our uninvited guest and see what he's up to," John said.

"Good idea, Son. I want to make sure there aren't any more unexpected surprises waiting for us."

Having someone else besides Sarah that he could trust with his secret, brought Peter a sense of comfort; and like he promised, John began doing some poking around of his own concerning Winston's death and his nephew's agenda. Franklin spent most of his time and money on gambling, drinking and whores; so, it was no surprise that his well was about to run dry. He had not anticipated being in North Carolina for this long, and the little money he had was disappearing fast. Franklin had always been a loser, a conman looking for the next big score; and Peter knew if he dug deep enough, he could dig a grave to bury Franklin alongside his uncle.

Knowing that foolish men sometimes bear their souls during pillow talk, especially after being baptized in whiskey, John decided to talk to one of the whores that Franklin frequented. Naomi was a sultry siren with long black hair and a curvaceous body. Her deep blue eyes were almost hypnotic and had put more than a few men in a trance; so, John was sure she would have information he could use. He entered the saloon that doubled as a brothel and went to meet Naomi. He knocked on her room door and waited, being careful not to be seen. Expecting that it was another customer, Naomi opened the door wearing only her bra and panties.

"Well hello gorgeous, you so handsome I'd do you for free," Naomi said with a seductive smile and distinct southern drawl.

Smiling at the compliment, John walked into the room. "Tempting offer darling, but that's not what I'm here for." John took a seat on the chair.

"Is that right? Then what can I do for you?" Naomi asked, lying across the bed.

"I hear you have a frequent customer these days, by the name of Franklin Dubois," John stated.

Naomi sat up on the bed and crossed her legs. "Ah yes, the fella from New Orleans; what's your interest in him?" she quizzed.

"Let's just say I'm very interested in what you two talks about." John responded.

With a laugh, Naomi said, "Talking ain't exactly what men are interested in when they come see me, handsome."

Taking money out of his pocket to show he was willing to pay for her information, John replied

"Well I sure would be grateful if you let me know if that changes; I'll be in touch to see if it does."

Looking at the amount of money John was willing to pay for information, Naomi quickly agreed to keep a listening ear.

"Sure, thing sugar; for that kind a money I will have him confessing like I was his priest," she said, eyeing the money

"Thank you darling," John said with a smile, then put the money on the dresser and left.

John knew his next visit would be more fruitful. One thing is certain, adding a little money to the mix goes a long way motivating people to give you what you want; and he could see the dollar signs in Naomi's eyes when he walked in the door. She was no fool and she knew that her discretion could go a long way in lining her pockets; and the money John offered for information was more than she made sleeping with 20 men. It didn't take a genius to figure out Naomi would be fully vested in siphoning information from Winston.

It didn't take long for John's investment to pay off. The very same night he put Naomi on the payroll, Franklin came in for his usual visit. This time, Naomi plied him with whiskey and massaged his shoulders, so he could relax. She played the role as if she was the dutiful housewife asking her husband about his day. As Naomi massaged and Franklin drank, he started to loosen up; and before he knew it, he was telling Naomi all about why he was really there.

Franklin said that he had blown all his money gambling and had gone to his uncle Winston's to see if he would give him a loan. When he arrived, he was told that Winston had been acting strange the week he left; and was walking around the house muttering about going to North Carolina to expose the Devereux's secret, but he never said what the secret was about. Thinking that the secret could be profitable, Franklin decided to hang around and wait for his uncle, but after he didn't return, he decided to come to North Carolina himself and find out what was going on.

When he arrived, he started asking questions about his uncle's whereabouts and found that he had rented a room in town. Further digging uncovered that Winston had been asking about the Devereuxs; and stated he was going to see them, but never returned. This prompted Franklin to pay the Devereuxs a visit in hopes that he could find out what happened to his uncle; as well as the secret Winston knew that could possibly yield a profit for them both.

When Franklin had no luck on his visit to the Devereuxs, he pressured the Sheriff to look into his uncle's disappearance. Just when it seemed that no explanation was in sight and Franklin's cash was almost gone, the Sheriff told him that Winston's body was discovered in a lake by the Devereux's property. Franklin figured he could use this news to blackmail the Devereux's into paying him off if he could link his uncle's murder to them. Now all he needed was the autopsy report to back up his claims. As Franklin continued to rattle on about his plans to fleece the Devereuxs, Naomi was making sure she took good mental notes. She knew this conversation was going to pay off for her.

Later that week, John returned to see how well his investment paid off. He knocked at the door, but this time Naomi answered covered in a robe. She knew that John wasn't there for her sexual services and that what he was interested in didn't require her to take off her clothes.

"Evening handsome; come on in and take a seat." Naomi said, ushering John in the door.
Taking a seat John said, "So what do you have for me?"

Naomi sat down and started telling John everything Franklin had said to her that night. She detailed everything he had planned and what he knew and didn't know. Pleased, John left Naomi another stack of money on the dresser.

"Nice work; I trust I don't have to tell you that this conversation stays between us?" John asked, watching Naomi count her considerable payment.

"My lips are sealed, handsome. I answer to only you," Naomi said, putting her new payment away.

"Smart girl; if you play your cards right, I may call on you in the future if I need your services again," John said, looking down at the beautiful vixen.

"And I am at your service, day or night." Naomi said with sincerity.

Smiling, John left the room knowing he had just made a valuable friend.

When John arrived at home, he filled his father in on all the details of Franklin's plan. Now that they knew what he was planning and what he knew, they knew how to stop him. The next day Peter paid a visit to the doctor to find out the results of Winston's autopsy. Although it was not procedure for the doctor to discuss the findings with someone that could be under suspicion of murder, Peter was a well-respected member of society with considerable power and wealth, so exceptions were made on his behalf.

"Hello doc, I was wondering if I might have a moment

of your time," Peter said, entering the doctor's office.

"Certainly Mr. Devereux, how may I be of assistance?"

the doctor replied. He then offered Peter a seat.

"Thank you, doc, you see I just haven't been able to sleep, wondering what happen to poor Winston. I mean with his body being found on my property I feel somewhat responsible for his untimely demise. So, I was wondering if you could help set my mind at ease and let me know what happened to him." Peter inquired with contrived concern.

"I understand Mr. Devereux. When I examined Mr. Dubois I found that there was no water in his lungs even though he had been submerged in the water for weeks; and there were small puncture wounds about the neck, face and torso," the doctor replied.

Looking confused, Peter said, "Doc I'm a businessman not a doctor, so could you tell me what all that means?"

"Sorry; it means that since there was no water in the lungs, Mr. Dubois was dead before he hit the water. The only injuries I found were the small puncture wounds that were consistent with snake bites," the doctor replied.

"Snake bites? Snakes killed Winston?" Peter asked, feigning surprise.

"That's certainly how it looks. Mr. Dubois seemed to have happened upon a nest of them, judging from the amount of bites. The large amount of venom stopped his heart and he likely stumbled into the water. So, you see, you have no reason to feel guilty Mr. Devereux. Mr. Dubois' death was just a tragic accident," assured the doctor.

Feeling more confident now, Peter said, "Thank you doctor, I really appreciate your time."

Shaking Peter's hand, the doctor replied, "No problem Mr. Devereux, the Sheriff will have my report later today."

Peter thanked the doctor again and left his office. Good, now I just have to wait for the sheriff to declare Winston's death an accident and get his parasite of a nephew out of town, Peter thought. He headed home to tell John the good news.

The Calm Before the Storm

Fall 1857

Now that Peter knew that Winston's death was going to be ruled an accident and John had discovered Franklin's real purpose for being in North Carolina; he felt he had the upper hand. He began to relax and even became more involved in the planning of his grandson's first birthday. Peter began ordering the best toys for a baby that money could buy; and making sure that all of the crème de la crème of North Carolina's high society received invitations to his grandson's unusual themed event. The way he saw it, this business with Franklin would be over sooner than later, then he could move on with his life; and it didn't take long for that vision to start to materialize.

October was now upon them; and it was a balmy Friday afternoon when Sheriff Gordon came to the Devereux plantation to deliver the news about Winston's autopsy. Since Peter already knew the results, he wasn't worried.

"Good afternoon Mr. Devereux," Sheriff Gordon said as he approached Peter, who was sitting on his porch enjoying the breeze.

"Good Afternoon Sheriff, what can I do for you this fine day?" Peter said with a genuine smile.

"Well, I came to deliver the news about Winston Dubois' autopsy report," replied Sheriff Gordon.

"Well come on up and have a seat Sheriff; would you like some lemonade? Sarah just made a fresh batch," Peter asked.

"Oh no sir, that's quite alright. Thank you kindly, but I am only going to be here for a minute or two."

"Alright then, so what's the final word?" Peter quizzed.

"Well the report came in from the doc this morning saying that Winston died of snake bites," informed Sheriff Gordon.

"Snake bites? Oh my, how did that happen?" Peter asked with feigned concern.

"Well the doc seems to think he may have been lurking around your property and happened upon a nest of copperheads. The doc reckons since there was so many of 'em, the amount of venom stopped his heart and he fell over in the lake. It's the damndest thing I ever seen. Poor bastard just had some bad luck, I guess. In any case we are ruling that the death was an accident and the case is being closed. We already told his nephew, so you shouldn't have any more trouble outta him. In fact, I kindly suggested that he move on back to New Orleans, so he can take care of his uncle's affairs,"

Sheriff Gordon stated with a sly grin.

Pleased that he wouldn't have to worry about how he was now going to get rid of Franklin, Peter replied, "Thank you so much Sheriff. I'm glad that this matter has been taken care of. Damn shame about old Winston, I guess he should have been more careful."

Nodding his head in agreement, Sheriff Gordon responded, "Indeed; well I better be getting back to town. I just didn't want this whole mess to keep hanging over your head. I know you're getting ready for your grandson's first birthday party and all. Ms. Helena has been in town buying up all kinds of stuff; I hear it's supposed to be some kind of Halloween theme. I bet that is gonna be something to see!"

With a genuine smile of pride, Peter said, "Yes, it is; and I hope you and your family will join us."

Surprised at the invitation, Sheriff Gordon stammered, "Well…sure, we'd love to be there."

"Great! I will make sure the invitation is sent to your office," Peter exclaimed.

Sheriff Gordon said his goodbyes and headed back to his office. Peter went inside and told John and Sarah the good news, then got back into the preparations for his grandson's party. Peter had remembered that there were some antique items in the closet of one of the rooms. He saw them as they were moving in their belongings, but had not had a chance to go through them. He thought it might be nice to see if there were any family heirlooms that he could pass down to John Jr.

Since Helena wanted to do something with a Halloween theme, he also knew he might find some things that could be used for décor. Uncle Thaddeus was considered by some to be worse than the devil himself so maybe he left his pitchfork behind. Peter chuckled to himself as he imagined old Thaddeus dressed up in red with a pointy tail and horns. Returning his attention to the mission at hand, Peter searched through box after box of dusty mementos and trinkets; he came across a journal that strangely, looked just like one that belonged to his wife Elizabeth and a letter addressed to him. Perplexed, Peter took the journal and letter into his room, so he could comfortably read them. He opened the letter first and saw that it was from his Uncle Thaddeus.

Dear Peter,

I found your wife's diary at your house during my visit. I am not sure what compelled me to read it, but I did; and when I read the contents I couldn't believe my eyes. I knew that if anyone else had found this journal, it would bring nothing but scandal. So, I took it with me when I left to protect you from the truth. Now that I have had time to sit with my suffering from this dastardly illness, I realize that it was not my secret to keep; it's yours I am truly sorry for any inconvenience or dismay I caused you and your family.

My intentions were only to protect you and the Devereux name. I can only hope that my penance will gain me entrance to heaven, for it won't be long now 'til the good Lord calls me home. This is my last letter to you my dear nephew. I hope you enjoy the spoils of my labor; and find Tobacco Road a suitable new home.

Uncle Thaddeus

Peter's heart started pounding as his mind started racing with a myriad of thoughts. He feared to think what could have been in his wife's journal that would have prompted such a reaction from his uncle. Slowly, Peter opened the dusty journal and took a deep breath. As he began to read page after page of his wife's inner most thoughts, Peter suddenly discovered what his uncle was so desperate to hide from him and the rest of the world.

There in Elizabeth's old journal, she detailed her anguish over learning of her father Joseph DuPont's affair with a slave named Bess and the child that was created from that affair. A little mulatto named Elizabeth who her father's wife Jane unknowingly raised as her own. Bess and Jane were pregnant at the same time. Whispers had circled around the plantation that the baby Bess was carrying was Joseph's and the stress was taking its toll on Jane.

The night that Bess' water broke, the stress finally became too much, and Jane went into premature labor. The baby was not strong enough to survive outside the womb and died. Joseph knew his wife had been trying to have a child for years with no success; and the guilt he felt that she lost her baby because of his actions was too much to bear. He didn't have the heart to tell her, so he switched the babies telling Bess that it was her child that died at birth and giving the other child to Jane; a child that she named Elizabeth.

When Thaddeus read the diary, he knew that his nephew had married a black woman passing as white. Being a rabid racist, Thaddeus could not afford for anyone to find out that his family's pure blood had been tainted by slave blood, so he stole the diary but didn't destroy it. When he became ill and it was clear he was soon going to meet his maker, Thaddeus decided he had to make amends and come clean with everything he had done, including keeping the truth from his nephew.

As Peter closed the journal he felt like his heart was pounding out of his chest. He couldn't believe what he just read. He was married to a black woman passing as white, which meant his son John was also black. Peter felt dizzy. He was so focused on hiding the secret of his grandson's paternity, even moving his family to another state to hide it; not knowing there was another secret lurking in the shadows that could destroy them as well.

Peter couldn't think. He felt like the walls were closing in on him. He loved Elizabeth more than life itself and she betrayed him. He needed some air and time to think. He took the journal and locked it in his desk so that no one else would find it; little did he know that was another secret that Sarah also shared.

Peter was unaware that before the diary had even made it to Uncle Thaddeus' hands, Sarah had stumbled upon it. That faithful night of Uncle Thaddeus' visit, she came across the journal while searching for something to make the gris gris. She never breathed a word to a soul about what she saw, but she never forgot it either.

Peter went into the garden, which had become his refuge, to collect his thoughts. His emotions were fluid like the ocean and moved from feelings of betrayal and hurt, to feelings of empathy and loss. No matter how much Peter hated that his wife kept something like that from him, he understood her reasons. And no matter how mad he was at his discovery, it didn't cancel out the years of love he had for her.

In an instant, Peter was taking a journey down memory lane that included the day they met, their first kiss and their wedding day. He had never loved anyone as much as he loved Elizabeth; and suddenly he understood his son's circumstance way more than he ever imagined.

Standing there looking out at his extensive property, Peter began to cry. Everything he thought he knew about his life and the people he loved was a lie; and all the people that he loved more than life were considered non-human by society's standards. Peter felt like he needed to escape from his own body; like even his skin was causing him to be claustrophobic. The feeling became too much for him and he just lay down on the ground and sobbed, watering his garden with his tears.

Peter lost track of time and place and soon was being roused by Nathaniel who was tending to the garden. "You aight Masta Devereux?" Nathaniel said with concern.

Peter shielded his eyes and looked up at Nathaniel's large dark frame. From Peter's vantage point on the ground, Nathaniel looked like a giant and almost eclipsed the sun.

"I'm fine Nathaniel; I guess I just got too hot and fainted." Peter lied.

"You want me ta fetch the doc fo ya?" Nathaniel asked, looking Peter over.

Embarrassed to be found lying in the garden, Peter replied, "No, I'll be fine Nathaniel; I'm just gonna go on up to the house and lie down for a bit."

Nathaniel helped Peter to the house and up to his room. Before he left, he told Peter he would have Sarah bring his dinner up to him later on. Peter thanked Nathaniel for helping him in the house and asked that he keep his little nap in the garden between them. Nathaniel agreed and left Peter to rest.

Although he was lying down, his rest was not a peaceful one. He was still plagued by thoughts and memories of Elizabeth; and of the son and grandchildren that shared blood from a slave. Just as he was immersed in his thoughts, Marie entered the room carrying Thomas Jr.

"I'm so sorry Master Devereux; I didn't know you were in here. I left the duster in here this morning and I was just gonna get it," Marie said.

Marie was startled to see Peter in his room at this time of evening. Peter looked at his grandson who was smiling at him as if he knew who he was; and in that moment, he noticed just how much he looked like John.

"Marie, is it ok if I hold him for a while?" Peter asked, still mesmerized by the toddler who was now giggling and reaching for him.

Surprised by his request, Marie responded, "Umm sure Master Devereux," and handed the baby to Peter.

Peter smiled as his grandson laughed at the funny faces he made for him; and when he put his tiny hands on Peter's face. He was so engrossed in playing with TJ that he didn't even notice the confused look on Marie's face. Peter had never held TJ before or even paid that much attention to his presence, so his sudden desire to play with him was more than unusual.

"Are you feeling alright Master Devereux?" Marie asked, still looking perplexed.

"I'm fine Marie; just fine." Peter said through smiles and tears. "Somebody has a first birthday coming up. Yes they do; yes, they do." Peter said to the excited toddler. Then without looking away from his grandson, Peter said "Marie, I'm so sorry for everything you have gone through at the hands of this family; and I promise you some things are gonna change."

Not knowing how to respond or even if Peter would hear her response, Marie kept silent. She didn't know what had gotten into Peter, but she was touched by the apology. Over the next several weeks, the plantation was buzzing with questions about what had gotten into Peter. He had been walking around in a daze like he was off in his own world. He started spending a lot of time in his room and he was spending a lot more time with both of his grandsons. Peter knew that he had to be very careful about what he let be known about his family, but the state of slavery began to leave an even more bitter taste in his mouth. He didn't know how he was going to do it, but he promised Elizabeth that he was going to take care of their family; all of them.

As the birthday party for John Jr. fast approached, the plantation was busy preparing for the grand event; and Peter was wishing that he had never planned the party in the first place. Now he wished for a small family affair that would celebrate both of his grandson's births equally; and he knew as liberal as he was known to be, celebrating the twins' birthdays together in a grand fashion would raise more than a few suspicions. So, he went ahead with the festivities as planned but made sure that he planned another private celebration that would honor TJ as well.

The day of the party, the plantation looked like a toddler wonderland. The finest trimmings and Halloween ornaments adorned every pillar and post. Helena had ordered decorations from all the finest shops and every baby toy imaginable was now lining the parlor floor. She ordered the finest custom-made costumes for her, John and John Jr. They looked the part of the perfect affluent southern family; flawless and beyond reproach. She wanted everyone that was invited to attend the party to be envious of the Devereux's status and wealth.

As the guests began to arrive, it looked as if they were attending a royal masquerade ball. The women, men and children were all impeccably dressed in their costumes and each arrived with an expensive gift for the young man of honor's big day. Marie looked on from the kitchen as she watched her son be treated like royalty. Being the biological mother of John Jr., this experience was bitter sweet. Her heart was filled with joy to see how happy he was and that everyone was bringing gifts fit for a young prince; but her heart was also breaking because her other son TJ would not receive the same. Even though they shared the same birthday and parents, they did not share the same life. There would be no grand celebration for TJ.

The wealthy white folks of North Carolina wouldn't line up to shower him with adoration and expensive gifts. No custom-made clothing or confection would symbolize the day of his birth. He was by society's standards the son of a slave and therefore his life was not worthy of celebration.

Marie continued to tend to her duties and ensure the guests were comfortable and enjoying the party. She tried to focus on the positive aspects of the day. No matter what society said or thought, to Marie, both her sons were princes to be adored. Although TJ's celebration would not be as grand as John Jr, Marie and her family had planned to have a party that would be just as special.

The day moved on and the party began to wind down. Guests gave their well wishes to the young Master Devereux and his parents, and then bid their adieus. Once everyone was gone, Marie and Sarah came in to prepare to clean up. To their surprise Peter instructed them to have a seat. Looking at each other with puzzled faces neither knew what was going on. Apparently, no one knew what to expect from Peter lately, so John and Helena were equally as bewildered.

As everyone sat in anticipation of what Peter was up to, his intentions soon became very clear. Peter returned to the room with TJ in tow. To everyone's astonishment, TJ was wearing the same type of custom made toddler costume that his brother donned earlier; and Peter was carrying a tray with a custom baked cake bearing the words Happy 1st Birthday TJ. The entire room was quiet at first because they were understandably in shock; but little did anyone know; Peter's day of surprises was just beginning.

Peter called all the slaves into the grand parlor to help celebrate TJ's birthday. None but the house slaves had ever even been inside of the main house, let alone been invited to stop working and celebrate something alongside the family. The slaves Peter brought with him to Tobacco Road were used to Peter being more laissez-faire than most slave masters, but even they were taken aback by the invitation. Though no one said anything, everyone was wondering what was going on with Peter; most wondered if he was even losing his mind. Lucid or loony, the slaves were not about to question a gifted opportunity to leave the fields and get a glimpse of life in the main house.

Each slave gladly attended the impromptu birthday party for baby TJ; and they brought along the gifts they had made for him. Although she still questioned Peter's sanity, Marie put those thoughts aside to enjoy her son's birthday. She could never remember being so happy; and John was grateful to have the opportunity to celebrate his other son's birthday as well.

By this point, Sarah had filled Jacob and Nathaniel in on the true identity of John Jr. and convinced them not to murder Peter in his sleep for his part in the task. For a moment it seemed as if they were all in a wonderful dream where slavery was non-existent; and all men were on equal footing. However, no slave let that moment sit in their mind for more than a moment. They welcomed and appreciated the opportunity they were given, but they were not by any stretch of the imagination– free.

The party goers began to get into the spirit of the day   as they watched TJ tear the wrapping from his gifts and show his new toys to his brother. The two children squealed and giggled as they played with each other and enjoyed the attention of the adults in the room. After TJ opened his gifts, everyone sang happy birthday to him and clapped as Marie and Thomas helped him blow out the candles. In true toddler fashion, TJ reached down and grabbed a tiny handful of the delectable confection and shoved it in his mouth.

Everyone laughed and got lost in the novelty of the day. Helena thought it was reprehensible that a slave child be dressed in the same fashion and receive the same treatment as an heir; but time and experience had taught her those thoughts are best kept to herself. No for the moment, she was quiet and didn't make a scene; but she was certain at that very moment that her father-in-law had taken leave of his senses. Now she just had to figure out how far off the cliff he had fallen; and what other lunacy he had in store.

The Storm

Spring 1858

After Peter's erratic behavior at the twin's birthday parties, Helena knew that something wasn't right; she just had to figure out what it was. She watched and scrutinized Peter's every move over the next few months to try to figure out what was going on with him; and she wasn't the only one. Everyone in the house was wondering what was going on with Peter and what had prompted his sudden dramatic shift in behavior. Even John wondered what was behind his father's new attitude; so, he decided it was time for a father son chat.

Spring was just beginning so John knew he would find Peter in what had become his favorite place of late, the garden. Walking up to Peter, who seemed lost in thought, John said "Are you alright father?"

Turning to see John staring at him with a look of concern, Peter replied "Yes son, I am alright; just admiring my garden. You can learn a lot from a garden."

Intrigued by his father's answer John asked, "How so?"

With a smile, Peter pointed to a bushel of flowers with various colored blossoms and said "You see those flowers son? They are all different colors. Some of them have pink blossoms, some white and some yellow; they look like three different kinds of flowers, but they are all part of a group of plants called Jasmines. Jasmines have the sweetest fragrances that you could ever smell; and no matter the color of the blossom they all possess that capability."

Confused as to what his father's lesson on plants had to do with anything, John asked. "What are you trying to say father?"

With a slight laugh, Peter responded. "I'm saying that you can't judge a plant, or person by their color son. I know that for generations that is what we were taught; and we passed those lessons down to our children, but it isn't right. You cannot judge a person's potential based solely on color; because at the end of the day we are all plants of the same species, even if the color of our blossoms is different."

Peter seemed lucid and almost enlightened in his conversation he was having with his son. In fact, he couldn't remember having a more meaningful father son moment. As John listened to his father's explanation it became clear that he wasn't losing his mind at all, he was finding his humanity; now he needed to know what happened to cause this sudden transformation.

"I understand that sentiment better than anyone father; because of society's views and rules, I cannot acknowledge the woman I love or my children. You cannot possibly comprehend what that is like." John said in a melancholy voice with his eyes cast down.

Still looking out at the horizon, Peter replied "I understand it a lot better than you think son."
John raised his head in bewilderment of his father's last statement and inquired "You do?"

Feeling that his son had a right to know the truth, Peter decided to tell him about his latest discovery. "Son, I know you have questions about my recent behavior; and I feel that you above all people have a right to know its origin. I found your mother's journal amongst your Uncle Thaddeus' things along with a letter." Peter began.

Puzzled, John quizzed "What was Uncle Thaddeus doing with Mother's Journal?"

With a sigh Peter continued "He stole it when he visited us all those years ago."

John felt a nauseous feeling start brewing in the pit of his stomach. He knew that whatever his father was about to say was going to be catastrophic, but he had to know.

"Why would Uncle Thaddeus steal my mother's journal? He barely knew her; so, what could she possibly have to say about him?" John posed.

With eyes cast down towards the ground, Peter answered "It wasn't what she said about him that was of concern. It was what she said about herself."

Now tiring of the back and forth question and answer period John exclaimed "Father for God's sake just tell me the truth! What did my mother say that would warrant Uncle Thaddeus stealing her journal?"

Looking John in the eyes, Peter replied "Your mother was Black."

John stood in silent disbelief and looked as if his entire life had just flashed before his eyes. When he was again able to speak, he inquired "How? What? I don't understand. Grandma Jane and Grandpa Joseph were both white."

Placing his arms around his son's shoulders, Peter explained "Yes son they were both white, but Grandma Jane was not your biological grandmother."

John looked like he had been hit in the stomach with a boulder. "If Jane is not my grandmother, then who is she?" John quizzed.

Taking his son by the hand and leading him over to take a seat on one of the garden's benches, Peter dictated the whole sorted story of Elizabeth's birth.

"Your grandpa Joseph had an affair with a slave named Bess and she became pregnant with your mother. At the time his wife Jane was also pregnant. Jane had been trying to have a baby for a long time, but she kept miscarrying. She had heard the rumors around the plantation that Bess was pregnant with her husband's child and the stress alone wore on her health. She went into premature labor the night Bess gave birth to your mother.

Jane's baby wasn't strong enough to live outside her body that early; and it died." Peter recounted.

"Joseph knew that Jane wouldn't survive losing another baby, so he took your mother and gave her to Jane; and told Bess that it was her baby that died. I think Jane and Bess knew in their hearts that your mother was really Bess' child, but Jane wanted so desperately to have a child; and Bess' station of being of slave made them both live with the lie in silence."

Peter waited for his son to process the information before saying anything else. John sat in shocked silence for what seemed to be hours, before he finally spoke. As he did he started putting the pieces together of how this revelation affected other members of his family.

"So that means that you were married to a Black woman, the daughter of a slave; and I as her son am also Black. I am married to a woman that I hate because you wanted to hide the fact that I fell in love with a slave and we had children together! Yet you were married to a Black woman and had children with her!" John screamed.

Peter attempted to calm his son by placing his arms around him, but John jerked away.

"My mother was just as Black as Marie and only a shade lighter, but she lived the life of a socialite and Marie the life of a slave! I am treated as the heir to a life of prosperity and one of my son's shares the state of his mother. You so easily took one my sons from Marie and discarded the other as an expendable piece of property. Tell me father, will you do the same of me? Do you love me any less now that you know I am Black?" John spat angrily with tears now streaming down his face.

Attempting to assuage his son's anger, Peter whispered "Of course not! I love you with all of my heart and I loved your mother as well. This does not change my love for either of you, but what it does change is my feelings about what I have done. Son, I am so sorry for all that I have put you and Marie through; and I don't know how I am going to do it, but I am going to make sure that she and your children are taken care of."

Now putting his arm around his son, Peter said "I know that you don't want to hear this right now, but given the circumstances of the world we live in, keeping this a secret is the only thing we can do. It is not only a matter of keeping our fortune, but our very lives as well! If anyone finds out about your mother, you or your children, they will be lining up to string us all up by the end of a rope! Keeping this secret is the only way to keep this family safe; all of us, including you and your children."

Though the thought of continuing with this charade of a life made John sick to his stomach, he knew his father was right. His family was safest if this secret remained just that – a secret. He would just have to resolve to do what he could to make life as safe and comfortable for his family as he could; even if that meant he could never be with them. There was something strange in the air, John could feel it; and it wasn't just the wake of his father's revelation of his identity. No, it was something bigger. Something was brewing like the winds before a storm.

John walked around like a zombie for days after his father's confession; and this made Helena even more curious as to what exactly was going on in the Devereux family. Not being a trusted member of the clan, Helena was consistently kept in the dark about things; and she didn't see that changing any time soon. So, if she wanted to know what was going on she was going to have to find out on her own; and that is exactly what she had planned to do.

Helena searched around in drawers and cabinets when no one was around, looking for clues as to what had taken hold of her extended family, but to no avail. After weeks of nothing to explain John and Peter's strange behavior, Helena put her investigation to rest for a while; but she was still observing.

Soon the issues on the Devereux plantation took a back burner to a much larger matter. A few months later, On June 16, 1858, the air of change was becoming clearer. Abraham Lincoln delivered what was to be known as the House Divided Speech after accepting the Illinois Republican Party's nomination for senator.

Peter was sitting on the porch reading the newspaper and its coverage of the speech. A house divided against itself cannot stand. I believe this government cannot endure, permanently, half slave and half free. I do not expect the Union to be dissolved—I do not expect the house to fall—but I do expect it will cease to be divided. It will become all one thing or all the other. Either the opponents of slavery will arrest the further spread of it, and place it where the public mind shall rest in the belief that it is in the course of ultimate extinction; or its advocates will push it forward, till it shall become alike lawful in all the States, old as well as new— North as well as South.

I can feel the trouble coming; and it is almost guaranteed to end in bloodshed. God help us all! Peter thought as he placed the paper in his lap. He had been hearing rumblings that the institution of slavery was being threatened for years now. In the 1830s the Postmaster General began refusing to allow any mail carrying abolition pamphlets to even be delivered to south.

Since then the plethora of agreements, court rulings and uprisings indicated that this was only the beginning. Abraham Lincoln campaigned and lost against Senator Stephen Douglas, the Democratic Party candidate later that year in 1858, but that was not the last anyone would see or hear of him; and Peter knew it was also not the last time slavery would be challenged.

Time moved on and soon it was time for the Devereux family to celebrate Christmas. Peter knew that there were going to be dangerous times ahead, so he just wanted to put everything out of his mind for a while and celebrate the lives of his now 2-year-old grandchildren.

Since Christmas was a private affair and to be celebrated away from prying eyes; Peter celebrated with both of his grandchildren equally. He also celebrated with Marie, Thomas and their family as well. This made Helena even more infuriated, but she dared not breathe a word. Even the slaves were allowed to celebrate with their families. For as long as he could, Peter wanted to embrace the good times.

On Christmas Eve Peter gathered the whole family in the parlor to decorate the tree. The house was filled with the scent of fresh pine and Christmas cookies; and the sounds of music and laughter. Since Peter was more openly embracing both of his grandchildren, John was able to spend more time with them as well. However, he never tried to overshadow Thomas' role in his son's life. Thomas was a good father and John could not have asked for a better man to raise his son; and for that he was eternally grateful. In an odd sort of way, they were all one big family; and everyone seemed to be happy with that – everyone but Helena.

John sat at the Piano and began playing as Nathaniel led everyone in singing Christmas Carols. Laughter and love filled the rafters and it seemed they were in their own little world. The fire was crackling and emitting a soft orange glow that made the whole house feel warm. Sarah came in from the kitchen carrying a big tray of Christmas cookies and everyone settled in for Peter to read a story to the children. The twins laughed as Peter made funny faces to emphasize the story; and soon the toddlers were drifting off to sleep.

After placing the kids in their beds, everyone settled in for the night. John was so happy that he went to bed with a smile as big as his children's. Helena took this as an opportunity to voice her opinion of the "new" Devereux family values.

"John, don't you think it strange that all of a sudden your father is behaving like the slaves are equal to us? I mean it's one thing to allow them a day to spend with their families out of the kindness of our hearts, but he is taking it to the extreme. Imagine a world where Negros and Whites were eating and socializing with one another; what kind of world would that be?" Helena said looking at John still laying with his back to her.

Without even turning around, John replied "A better one."

Sensing that she would get no support from her husband, Helena tabled the discussion for the night and went to sleep.

The next day everyone woke to the smell of the huge Christmas breakfast that Sarah had cooked. One by one, the family came downstairs and took a seat at the table; to Helena's surprise Marie and her family were also seated at the table. The look on her face was enough to show that she did not approve, but in case there was any doubt, she voiced that disapproval as well. The sight of Marie and everyone she viewed to be less than she was, sitting at the table as if it was their right, was too much for her to swallow.

"I have had enough!" Helena shouted slamming her hand down on the table.

Everyone stopped and turned to see what Helena was going to do next. When she had everyone's attention Helena continued "Father Devereux, have you and John taken leave of your senses? Slaves sitting at the table with us, celebrating holidays with us; what's next? Are you going to grant them their freedom as well? This is very inappropriate, and I will not stand for it! Marie and her family are to be removed this instant!" she demanded.

Peter's jaw tightened as he watched Helena's little floorshow. It had been a long time since he had to let her know who the head of the family really was, so he thought maybe she needed to be reminded. He was not about to tolerate any of her antics today and his patience with her had grown very thin over the years. At times he regretted even coming up with that whole idea with her father, especially since Uncle Thaddeus' money had given him the same power and prestige in North Carolina that he sought in New Orleans.

Not wanting to scare the children any further than Helena's outburst already had, Peter said through a feigned smile. "Helena darling, I am going to assume that you have just taken leave of your senses and temporarily forgot that I am the head of this family, not you. So why don't you just have a seat and enjoy your food."

Defiant, Helena says "I will not sit down and eat breakfast with slaves!"

Having had enough of Helena's tantrums, Peter says with continued smile "Everyone go back to enjoying this lovely breakfast that Sarah prepared and I'm gonna have a little talk with my daughter in law in the other room."

Peter took Helena in the kitchen and spun her around to face him. The fire in his eyes made Helena start to rethink her previous course of action. "Let me tell you something little girl, I have had it with your blatant disregard for my house and my decisions. Lest you forget whose roof you sleep under my dear, you may find yourself sleeping outside in the slave quarters. Imagine how close you will be then. I suggest you get use to change darling, because as best I can tell, it's coming; and there ain't nothing any of us can do to stop it." Peter stated and returned to the table to rejoin his family. The rest of the day went on without incident and that peace continued on through New Year's.

Although life on the Devereux plantation was calm, the rest of the world was in unrest. The fighting over slavery began to get worse and it seemed war was eminent. The entire year of 1859, everyone lived on edge as stories of uprisings and unrest filled the streets. The most chilling was when White American revolutionary abolitionist John Brown was executed for his parts in leading the 1856 Pottawatomie Massacre in Bleeding Kansas; and a raid at Harpers Ferry in 1859. His last coup was unsuccessful and led to his being executed on December 2, 1859. News of his death symbolized the beginning of a new era.

There was no sign that the issue of slavery was going to die down and everything pointed to the situation only getting worse. Both sides of the issue seemed to be standing their ground and neither seemed open to compromise. At this point it was a standoff; and Peter was nervous about what was going to happen next. The answer to his question came when the once defeated Abraham Lincoln was running for President of the United States in the 1860 election.

Southern states had threatened to secede if he was elected and in November of 1860, the South's worse nightmare come true. Lincoln being elected president was the final straw for southern states; after that, all hell broke loose, and Peter was faced with the realization that his family's lives were now in real danger.

War

Spring 1861

After Lincoln's election in 1860, the world seemed to be in chaos. By February 7, 1861 seven slave states had seceded from the United States and adopted a provisional constitution for the Confederate States of America. An American Statesman named Jefferson Davis was serving as their President. Lincoln took office on March 4, 1861 and in his inaugural address he declared that any secession from the Union was "legally void". He said that he had no intention of ending slavery in the states where it already existed, nor did he intend to invade them; but he would use any means including force, to maintain federal property.

Lincoln rejected the South's offer to buy the federal properties and enter into a peace treaty with the United States, because he said they were not a legitimate government. So, Davis demanded that Ft. Sumter (which was still held by the union, but located in the middle of the harbor in Charleston,

South Carolina) be surrendered.

Neither the outgoing Buchanan administration nor the incoming Lincoln administration, would agree to turn over the fort; and the Confederate government refused a conditional reply given by Union Maj. Anderson.

On April 12, 1861, Davis ordered that the fort be attacked. The attack lasted for two days before the fort finally surrendered on April 13, 1861. Lincoln responded with a call for 75,000 troops from the Union states to bring back federal property and recapture the fort. However, North Carolina, Virginia, Arkansas and Tennessee decided to join the seceded southern states instead of sending troops to help attack them. In turn, the Northwestern part of Virginia chose to secede from Virginia and joined the Union as the new state of West Virginia.

Later that month Lincoln announced what was to be known as the Anaconda Plan, in which all southern ports were blocked, and commercial ships were no longer able to get insurance. He called it the Anaconda plan because its purpose was to squeeze the South's economy to death. This caused the South's cotton trade to be seriously impacted which infuriated the southern states even more. Only Kentucky tried to remain neutral and not join either side; but in September of 1861, Confederate forces invaded the state and Kentucky joined the Union States, while still trying to maintain slavery.

The war caused hundreds of thousands of young men to rush to enlist; it was considered a great honor to go to war to defend their way of life. However, as the war dragged on the eagerness began to disappear; and a draft was implemented in 1862 by both the Union and the Confederate states to increase numbers. The only people exempt from the draft were members of the clergy, government and overseers.

This news made Peter very anxious, John was his only son and he did not want to lose him. Nor did he want him to be forced to defend a way of life that by all intents could have kept him in bondage if the truth was known. John was also uneasy; he did not want to fight for the south and he was nervous about what would happen to his family if he did get drafted to war. Who would protect them? What would happen if he was killed? The thought of fighting for a way of life that oppressed his family made him sick to his stomach. He had decided that if drafted, he was going to flee to Canada.

"You look nervous." Helena said as she came upon John pacing back and forth in their room.

"Have you no idea what is going on right now? There is a war going on Helena and they have begun drafting men into the military to fight; which means that in all likelihood I may be drafted as well!" John said still pacing back and forth.

With a sarcastic grin, Helena replied "Well you shouldn't have to be drafted. I can think of no greater honor than going to battle to defend our way of life."

With obvious agitation, John retorted "Then why don't you sign up? You most certainly wouldn't be missed. In fact, I can think of no greater honor than hearing that a union soldier had separated your head from your neck. Maybe then you wouldn't be able to irritate me with your incessant babbling and asinine remarks!"

Offended, by her husband's stinging comments Helena retaliated. "Of course, you don't want to defend our way of life, because if you had your way you would be allowed to marry your nigger whore and live happily ever after! Well I am sorry to say, that is not what God intended; and this little coup by the Union to impose their hedonistic ideals on us is going to fail! I don't know what you ever saw in her anyway, she's a slave, she is property meant to serve a purpose as all property is meant. She and her children are no better than the cows or mules in the pasture. You should be glad that I am a good Christian and accepted your little bastard son. For that alone you should wrap your arms around me and thank me!"

Helena was so engrossed in her soap box speech that she didn't even see John's expression change. Before she knew it, John had charged her and pinned her against the wall with his hands around her throat. "How about I just wrap my hands around your throat and squeeze until your windpipe collapses?" John spat.

A surprised Helena clawed at John's hands saying "John what are you doing? You're choking me? I can't breathe."

Sarcastically John responded "Oh I thought you wanted me to wrap my hands around you to show my appreciation. See the problem with you Helena, is you just don't know when and how to stop talking. So, I figure if I help you stop breathing, maybe we can cure that little problem."

Helena continued to fight for air and John continued to taunt her. "It would be so easy for me to kill you right now, but lucky for you, you are not worth it. But if you ever insult Marie or my children again, I will change that opinion." John warned as he released his grip on Helena.

Helena collapsed to the ground coughing and holding her throat. It took her a minute to catch her breath; and when she did, she dared not use it to utter another word to John. Instead she sat down and tried to process what just happened. Helena was visibly shaking. She and John had argued before, but never had he put his hands on her. She knew that something in him had definitely changed and thought it was best that she put some distance between her and the Devereuxs. Helena packed her bags and planned to leave for New Orleans to visit her parents.

As Helena packed, Marie came in to straighten the room. "Oh, I'm sorry Miss Helena; I didn't know anyone was in here. I will come back later." Marie said and turned to leave.

Helena didn't respond, but Marie noticed that Helena was packing. "Are you going somewhere Miss?" Marie asked.

Not bothering to look at Marie, Helena responded. "Yes, if you must know, I am going to visit my parents in New Orleans for a little while."

With genuine concern Marie stated "Oh no Miss; I don't think that is a good idea. They are fighting out there and you may get caught in the crossfire or worse. It's too dangerous to travel now."

Looking at Marie with disdain, Helena retorted "I beg your pardon? You dare tell me what I should do or what you think? Contrary to the way you are treated around here sweetheart, you are nothing more than a slave. So, by definition, you can't think nor form an opinion. Now please excuse yourself and tell that husband of yours to prepare the carriage and get ready to take me to my destination."

Marie looked down at the floor and said, "My apologies Miss; I will fetch Thomas." Marie exited the room without another word.

Peter got wind of Helena's travel plans and her order to have Thomas accompany her. He entered her room and found her just closing her suitcase. "Do you mind telling me what the hell you think you are doing?" Peter asked catching Helena off guard.

"Father Devereux, you startled me". Helena said placing her hand over her chest.

"What is this that I hear about you taking a trip to New Orleans and having Thomas to drive you in the carriage?" Peter inquired.

Composing herself, Helena answered "Yes, I thought I would go and visit my parents for a little while."

Peter looked at Helena in disbelief and said "Are you insane? There is a war going on out there and you think that now is a good time to take a trip to New Orleans? You are not about to do something that foolish. Now put down your bags."

Standing her ground, Helena said "No offense Father Devereux, but you don't own me, so you can't tell me what to do."

With an astonished expression, Peter replied "No, you are right you may come and go as you please. So, if you want to go, be my guest. But for all intents and purposes, I do own Thomas and the carriage that you are using, so THEY will not be going anywhere."

Knowing that Peter had successfully put Helena in her place, he turned to leave. Before he exited the room, he turned and offered in sarcastic tone "You have a safe trip now you hear? And do tell your lovely parents I said hello."

Looking dejected, Helena sat down on the bed. If she was to get to New Orleans, she was going to have to find another way. The next morning, Helena rode into town with the mail carrier when he came to deliver the Devereux's mail. From there she caught a ride with a man by the name of William Mumford. Mumford was a native to North Carolina, but now resided in New Orleans. He was returning home and happily allowed Helena to travel with him. He didn't think it wise for a woman to travel that distance alone.

Upon their arrival in New Orleans, Helena thanked the kind stranger and made her way to her parent's plantation. Days later, Union Navy ships descended on New Orleans. Helena would later learn that her travel companion Mr. Mumford would be tried for tearing down an American flag that was hung by the Union soldiers. He was executed on June 7, 1862 in the courtyard of the Mint from which he tore down the flag.

Back in North Carolina, no one was concerned that Helena had left. Given everything that was going on, it was a sigh of relief not to have her snooping around digging for dirt. Helena's absence left room for the family to focus on more important matters, like what was going on with this war and how they were going to be impacted. Battle stories from the war continued to circulate around North Carolina plantations and one caught Jacob's attention. When he was on an errand in town to gather some supplies, he heard some other slaves talking about an escaped slave named Robert Smalls, who had become a war hero by turning over a Confederate steamer called The Planter to the Union Navy.

"Ah man that's just a tale; ain't no white man gon let a slave fight in their military!" a short older slave said laughing at a story another younger slave was telling about Robert Small's exploits.

The younger slave was tall and strong with skin the color of midnight; and he was not affected in the least by the older slaves taunting. The younger slave defended his story replying "It is true! Robert Smalls is a hero and he even got a reward bounty from President Lincoln himself! He is a real war hero; and he even got permission from President Lincoln to raise a Negro regiment for the Union."

The older slave continued to laugh and said "Sho he did young buck" as he went on his way. The old man could not conceive what the young slave was talking about, but Jacob certainly did.

"Hey what was that you were telling that old man about a Negro Army?" Jacob asked.

The young man turned around to see an eavesdropping Jacob standing behind him. "I don't know you man, you may be one of those slaves run back and tell your massa everything. I don't know nothing." The young man said.

"I ain't no turncoat; and if they got a Negro regiment, I wanna join!" Jacob said careful not to let his voice be heard. The young slave looked at Jacob and saw that he was sincere.

"Name's Otis; what's yours?" the young man said looking around.

"My name's Jacob, Jacob Monet". Jacob said shaking Otis' hand.

Otis looked around to make sure that their conversation had not gain the attention of any onlookers and proceeded to pretend to be gathering supplies as he told Jacob the story. Otis filled Jacob in on the exploits of escaped slave turned war hero, Robert Smalls. Then, he told him about Smalls traveling to Washington to get permission from the President to raise the first black regiment; a request that was granted on August 25, 1862 by Secretary of War Stanton.

Jacob's eyes widened, as Otis told him a group of slaves were escaping to join the 1st South Carolina Infantry, under the command of Brigadier General Rufus Saxton. When Jacob confirmed that he wanted to go as well, Otis informed him of the meeting place and time. The two men said their goodbyes quickly and went their separate ways before anyone notice.

When Jacob returned home, he knew that he had to tell his parents and he also knew that it was not going to go well.

"You did what?" Sarah screamed in response to Jacob's announcement.

Standing his ground, Jacob said "I'm going to join the Union's first Black regiment. I am going to fight for our freedom."

Sarah pleaded with Jacob to reconsider. "Why would you do something like that? Baby I just got you back, I am not going to risk losing you again! This family has got to stay together!" She begged.
Jacob hated breaking his mother's heart, but he couldn't go back on his beliefs. "I love you Mama, and I am coming home to you a free man." Jacob stated.

"Who will look after you?" Sarah asked.

"I will." Nathaniel said.

Sarah looked at Nathaniel and began to sob. "No Nate! Sweet Jesus No! I lived without you all these years and I am not about to lose my husband and my son again. I won't make it!" She cried.

Suddenly, a voice came from behind them. "Miss Sarah is right Mr. Nate. You should stay here to help protect her, Marie and the kids. I will go with Jacob and look after him." Thomas stated.

Marie looked at Thomas and said, "No Thomas you don't have to do this."

Putting his arms around Marie, Thomas replied. "I am going to be fine baby. I am going to look out for your brother and we are both coming back home to you. You just take care of TJ and tell him his father loves him. This is something I have to do Marie. As a slave have no control of my destiny and my decisions are not mine; as a soldier I am fighting for my family to truly be free."

Marie knew there was no talking Thomas out of his decision and she resolved to just pray for his and Jacob's safe return. With news of the first Black regiment spreading across the country, many slaves fled to help them fight. To many, it was an honor to be able to wear a uniform and fight alongside White soldiers. They viewed it as their opportunity to fight for their own freedom.

As a slave you could have your dignity and your life taken from you at any time for any reason. Being able to join the military allowed a slave to use his life to preserve his dignity and the dignity of his race. Thousands of slaves wanted to take advantage of that opportunity, and Jacob and Thomas were no different.

Peter was aware of Jacob and Thomas' plan to flee and decided to help them. He knew trying to escape was going to put them both in danger from some other slave master catching them; and he would not have their death on his conscious. Peter knew that no would question his travels or suspect him of helping slaves escape, so he told them that he would transport them to South Carolina.

Peter would pose as if he was going to South Carolina on a business trip and take Jacob and Thomas with him. Once in South Carolina, he would get them as close to the camp as he could without being seen.

Peter threw a small celebration for them prior to their departure so everyone could wish them safe passage. They ate, drank and danced the night away; and before he brought the festivities to a close, Peter led everyone in a prayer. Everyone joined hands and bowed their head as Peter began "Father God, I come to you as your humble servant asking that you form a fiery hedge of protection around Thomas and Jacob. Protect them dear lord as they embark on this journey, and bring them back to us safely. This I ask in Jesus' name, Amen."

The party ended, and Jacob and Thomas prepared for bed. That night, they lay blankets on the floor, so they could all sleep next to each other. For their last night together, their family wanted them to know they were loved; and to remind them what they were fighting to come home to.

The next morning, they all ate breakfast as a family and said a final prayer for their departing soldiers. As Thomas was leaving, John ran up to bid him farewell. "You come back safe now you hear? Marie needs her husband and TJ needs his father." John said with sincere gesture. The twins were now 6 years old and TJ had grown extremely close to Thomas. Losing his own mother at 6, John knew if Thomas didn't return it would be a devastating loss for TJ.

Putting his hand on John's shoulder, Thomas said "If I don't come back, I need you to promise me that you will take care of them. In my absence I need you to be the husband and father they need."
With a nod of agreement, John pulled Thomas into an embrace to solidify his promise. Then Thomas and Jacob climbed aboard the carriage with Peter to leave. Their family stood there watching, waving and saying their goodbyes. Although Sarah was afraid for Jacob, she was proud he was now a man.

Chapter Sixteen

The Good, the Bad & the Ugly

Fall 1862

Peter's heart was thumping in his chest as he sat in the carriage, with Thomas and Jacob driving. He took a drink of whiskey to steady his nerves and rehearsed what he would say if he was stopped by any Confederate soldiers. Peter was aware of what would happen if he was caught helping slaves make it to the Union regiment. The country was in serious unrest; and an act of this nature would be viewed by his fellow southerners as treason, punishable by death.

Peter knew the only way to keep his family safe was to put on the performance of a lifetime; and be sure not to crack under pressure. Amazingly Peter made it to the Union Camp in South Carolina safely; and got Thomas and Jacob there undetected. He said his quick goodbyes to them both and left before he could be recognized.

Jacob and Thomas walked up to a tent that was set up to enlist new soldiers. They were signed in and given their instructions, then pointed to the tent they would be sharing to get settled in.

"I can't believe we're here." Jacob said looking at Thomas.

"Me either; who would have thought there would be a Negro regiment fighting in the war?" Thomas replied with a smile.

"Not me; but I sure am glad I get to be a part of it." Jacob said, and then looked at Thomas with his smile now faded. "Are you scared?" he said.

Thomas looked at Jacob. He could see the fear on Jacob's face and he knew he had to reassure him.

"Now don't you go getting nervous on me; we are out here because of you. You sold me on this dream of fighting to be free men and you can't back out now. We are gonna look out for each other; and we are gonna come home heroes, like that Smalls guy you were telling me about," Thomas said, playfully nudging Jacob, trying to calm his fears, then continued. "We are gonna be alright Jacob. God got a plan for us; that's why we here and no matter what happens we are gonna be free."

Jacob nodded in agreement and then he and Thomas put their things down and reported for duty. Jacob and Thomas were amazed at all the Black men they saw there to fight. A soldier named Louis Garrison or "Lou" as he liked to be called, was designated as their personal mentor in becoming accustomed to military life. He was a brown skinned man of medium stature from South Carolina; and was one of the Sea Island Blacks that were known as Gullah people.

Jacob and Thomas both liked Lou instantly; they mostly liked hearing him speak, even if it was difficult sometimes to understand him. Being Gullah, meant that Lou spoke a language known as Gee Chee, which was also the name Gullah people were called at times. It was an English based language that mixed African words and influences and sounded like a Jamaican, Barbadian or Bahamian dialect.

"Dis ober yah is da school. Una gonna learn ta be smaat yah," Lou said, pointing out the school that had been set up to teach the soldiers to read and write.

Jacob and Thomas both looked at each other in confusion as they tried to decipher what Lou was trying to say.

"Boy you sho talk funny!" Jacob said.

Laughing, Lou said, "Una get use ta it. Ma Mammy eh Gullah an she fuss taut me ta tawk; so sumtime ma Gee Chee com ot."

The men all shared a laugh and Lou made an extra effort to speak a little clearer as he went over the different drills and duties that everyone was to perform. He showed them how and when to salute and how to address a fellow soldier or their commander. The company was under the command of Colonel Thomas Wentworth Higginson and consisted of about 86 men. It was as if they had stepped into a dream; but it didn't take long for them to be reminded of the nightmare that could await them.

Thomas and Jacob listened intently, as Lou told them that even though they were officially Union soldiers, if they were captured by the Confederates they would likely be shot, even if they were trying to surrender. And if they were allowed to surrender, they would be enslaved. Jacob could not imagine being a slave again, especially not to the Confederates; he knew if it came down to that choice, he would choose death.

The next morning, they started their life as enlisted soldiers in the 33rd. USCT Company A: 1st South Carolina Infantry. The soldiers saw action on an expedition along the coasts of Florida and Georgia that lasted November 3-10, 1862: first on November 7 at Spalding's on Sapello River, Georgia, and then again on November 8, at Doboy River.

Thomas and Jacob managed to return from battle unscathed, but homesick. They knew they were there for the right reasons, but the approaching Thanksgiving holiday made both of them ache for home and family. When Christmas came, their longings for home became worse. For Thomas, he longed to spend the holiday with Marie and the boys; and he prayed each day that God would grant him safe passage home to them.

When the New Year came in, it signaled the beginning of a new era in American history. On January 1, 1863 Camp Saxton held a celebration in honor of President Lincoln's Emancipation Proclamation, which freed slaves in Confederate states. The soldiers were now officially free men; and they received their regimental colors and were officially paid for their service.

The feeling of pride felt by the men in that regiment was overwhelming; and Thomas and Jacob were grateful they were able to be a part of it.

For the first time, they felt like they were no longer slaves; they were soldiers.

The war continued, and back in North Carolina, John managed to avoid being drafted; but when Lincoln's Emancipation Proclamation went into effect, it was another development that would directly impact his family. Legally, Marie, their children, her parents and every other slave in Confederate states were now free. The very thing that Jacob and Thomas had risked their lives to fight for had come to pass; and John was as excited as the slaves on the plantation, but he was also scared about what was going to happen next. Hatred was something that had deep roots in the South and no law in world could change that.

When the news broke, slaves on plantations everywhere rejoiced. It was a happy day. No more bondage and the freedom to live their lives as they choose. That was the thought, but unfortunately not the reality, as news also spread about the mass lynching and other violent acts being committed.

Some slave owners were so evil, that they would rather see their slaves dead than let them go free. John was also afraid of what would happen if some renegade Confederate soldier started a killing spree rather than see slaves go free. It seemed no matter what new strides the country was making at racial equality and human decency, there was always going to be some that would fight against progress. When Marie heard the news of their emancipation, she jumped for joy and went to find her parents.

"Mama did you hear? We're free!" Marie shouted as she ran from room to room looking for Sarah. She found her mother and father standing in the parlor. Sarah was crying, and Nathaniel was holding her in his arms. Marie stopped in her tracks and her elation was replaced by a sinking feeling in the pit of her stomach.

"Mama, Papa, did you hear? President Lincoln set us free! We don't belong to nobody no more! We can do as we please and live as we please!" Marie shouted.

Sarah and Nathaniel both looked into the eyes of their optimistic daughter with broken hearts.

Putting his hands on his daughter's shoulders Nathaniel said "Lissen baby gal, even if da law say we free, white folks ain't gonna let no Negro be equal ta dem. Right nah, dere slave mastas killin' off dey slaves sted of let'em go."

Looking at her father with tears streaming down her face, Marie shouted, "No Papa! They can't do that. President Lincoln said we're free, they have no right. They have no right!"

Holding his daughter close in his arms, Nathaniel whispered, "White folks don't care 'bout whas right baby; an you mauk my wurds, thangs gonna git worse 'fo dey get better. Befo, lees we wus protected frum White folks hurtin us 'cause dey respected each udda's propty; an we wus dey propty. Nah anythang can happ'n, 'specially in da souf. White folks down heh so fulla hatred dey'd kill us jus 'cause we cross dey path. You be ca'ful baby; an keep ya eyes op'n. Deys sum dawk times ahead."

Marie sobbed in her father's arms, as Sarah wrapped her arms around their daughter as well. Though no one spoke for a while, each of them silently prayed for Thomas and Jacob's safety and return home. Finally, Marie broke the silence with the question that was on each of their minds. "Papa, now that we're free, does that mean the war is over and Thomas and Jacob can come home?"

Wiping his daughter's tears from her cheek, Nathaniel replied "I don't know baby gal. Les hope so."

Meanwhile Peter and John were having their own discussion about the recent news. "Father, did you hear the news? President Lincoln freed the slaves," John quizzed, walking into his father's room.

"Yes son, I heard. It's wonderful news," Peter responded. Looking at the concerned look on his father's face,

John asked, "If it's so wonderful, then why do you look so unsettled?"

Placing the Bible, he was reading down on the bed, Peter responded, "Because I have heard other news as well."

Taking a seat beside his father on the bed, John inquired, "What news?"

Peter looked down at the floor and replied, "The news about the hangings. When the Union Soldiers began coming around to the plantations informing people that the slaves were free, some slave masters got the word before the soldiers' arrival. The thought of letting the slaves go free was something they could not tolerate, so they started slaughtering as many as they could before the soldiers got there.

Men, women, children and whole families were gone in the blink of an eye. A man they discovered was passing for White was tarred and feathered." Peter's voice got lost in his sobs as he thought of what would be done to his son and grandson, if they were found to be passing as well.

John looked horrified, as the same thoughts ran through his mind. He could not bear it if anything happened to his family. The only living person that knew their secret who could be a threat was Helena and she was gone; but no matter where she was in the world, she was still a threat. The only thing that kept her from telling the truth about his son until now was her desire to punish Marie and perpetrate a fraud of having borne a Devereux heir.

John could not concern himself with Helena at the moment; he had to focus on what to do for any immediate threat. It was like a cruel joke; he couldn't be with his family because they were slaves, but now that they were free he could very well lose them forever. John and Peter decided they needed to make plans on how they were going to protect themselves and their family from any impending threat.

Elsewhere, Jacob and Thomas were again engaged in battle. On January 23, 1863 their company boarded the steamer, the John Adams Planter leaving Beaufort South Carolina headed up St. Mary's River to Georgia and Florida. The river itself was a dangerous enemy. It was bordered with high bluffs in some spots, which were ideal places for the enemy to hide and ambush them; and the stream was winding, narrow and swift, making it difficult to navigate. In spite of the river's treacherous conditions and the enemy's steady assault, they were continuously victorious against Confederate forces. But, it was on a midnight march at Township, Florida that they suffered a loss.

Since the day they met, Lou, Jacob and Thomas had vowed to always look out for each other; and they had kept that promise. On every expedition, against all odds, they fought for their country and they fought for each other; doing both successfully. The night of the march they started out like they had time and time again, with Lou in front, Jacob in the middle and Thomas in the back. Because Jacob was the youngest (though only by a year) it was instinct for Thomas and Lou to try to protect him.

As they marched through the pine woods they became completely surrounded by the Confederates. An attack ensued and the 33rd managed to fend off their enemy and drive them into the woods. Although the casualties were larger on the Confederate's side, the loss to Jacob was significant. When the dust had settled, and the enemy was successfully defeated, Jacob turned to see Thomas lying dead from a single shot to the head. His body was taken back to camp and buried, but before his body was laid to rest, they said a prayer for their fallen comrade; and Jacob cut off one of the insignias from his uniform as a memento of the brother he loved.

Jacob moved through the rest of his time in the 33rd like he was sleepwalking. Although Lou was still there for him, no one could replace Thomas. Jacob was consumed with guilt, because he felt that had it not been for him, Thomas would be home safe with Marie and their son. Oh Marie, how can I tell you that because of me your husband is dead; and how can I tell my nephew his father will never come home. Jacob pondered with a broken heart.

"Him free nah Jake; truly free. Him beyon dis worl of pain. Hona 'em an fight. Finis wat him stat," Lou said, trying to comfort Jacob. Through tear streamed eyes, Jacob pushed on, vowing to bring Thomas' insignias home to his sister.

Back in North Carolina things were getting steadily more dangerous; and Peter feared more and more for John and their family's safety. He knew that the only way they were going to be safe, was to leave North Carolina; and the only way they could actually be together would be to go to Canada. The latter was going to be extremely difficult, but Peter saw no alternative. He quietly started inquiring how he could get John, Marie and the twins to safety in Canada; and learned of an old minister who had helped hundreds of slaves escape to the North. Although the slaves were technically free now, Peter knew that John and his son being passers put them in serious danger; and that no matter where they went in the North, society would still never allow him and Marie to be together to raise their children.

The minister agreed to get John, Marie and the twins safely to Ohio; from there they would be transported across to Canada. In order for the plan to work, it would take some time and that was in short supply. Peter worked with the Minister to set up a safe place for John and his family to stay when they got there; and jobs as well. He accumulated a significant amount of cash for them to take to get them started. Now he just had to tell the rest of the family about the plan.

Peter gathered everyone in the parlor to discuss the plan. "I wanted all of you here because we have to make a decision. Things around here are getting very precarious and I don't think it's safe for you to stay here any longer. Now I've been talking to an old minister who used to be a part of the Underground Railroad and he said that he can help get you all to Canada."

Shaking her head, Sarah stood and said, "I'm not going anywhere without Jacob. When he comes home I'm going to be here. I will not leave my baby again."

Trying to convince her, Peter replied, "Now Sarah, I'll tell Jacob where you are and try to get him up there with you when he returns."

Sarah continued her stance. "No! I appreciate your offer Master Devereux, but…"

Interjecting, Peter responded, "Please call me Peter. I am not your master; we are family."

Sarah stopped midsentence. Although she knew about the twins being John's and about Elizabeth being the daughter of a slave, she was still surprised at this response.

Peter continued, "We've all been through too much together to keep secrets from each other any longer. John Jr and TJ are both my biological grandchildren and that's no longer a secret; but there's something else that you need to know as well. John's mother, my wife Elizabeth, was the daughter of a slave named Bess. She was given to her father's wife Jane to be raised as their child, the same way I took John Jr. to be raised by John and Helena."

The room got quiet. Sarah knew about John's mother, but she had never breathed a word to anyone; not even Nathaniel or Marie.

"What?" Marie said with an astonished look.

Peter turned to Marie. "My son is Black passing for White; the same as my grandson, and I love them both with all of my heart. I would die if any harm came to them and for that reason they cannot stay here. The Confederacy may be losing the war, but they are still just as dangerous as they would be if they were winning. People who are found to be passing as White are being lynched, burned and God knows what else. I will not take the chance on something happening to them!" Peter said with tears welling up in his eyes.

Marie collapsed on the couch in disbelief and Peter went to her on bended knee. "Marie, words can never express how sorry I am for all that you have suffered at the hands of this family; and there is nothing in this world I can do to make that up to you, but please at least let me try. Let me give you the life you should have had; a life with you and John raising your sons together freely." Peter begged, holding her hand.

Taking her hand away, Marie said, "I am a married woman Mr. Devereux. My husband is off fighting for his family and I will not abandon him.

When he and my brother return, they will find their family here waiting. I am staying with my mother and father. I'm not leaving!"

Peter knew that Marie could be stubborn, but he also knew that she, John and the babies had no choice but to leave; now he just had to make her see that, before it was too late.

What Doesn't Kill You

Summer 1864

Marie kept her word and refused to leave without her brother and her husband; and nothing Peter could say could convince her otherwise. There was a nervous energy surrounding the plantation and Peter could feel the threat getting closer to his front door. When the slaves had been emancipated, Peter let those who wanted to stay remain on as sharecroppers. Since he had not been a mean slave master, most of the slaves decided he may not be a bad landlord either, so they stayed.

Peter did not profit as heavily from share cropping as he had when he owned slaves, but the tradeoff for him was worth it. He never really cared for the system of slavery in the first place; and over the course of his life he had amassed a fortune that would sustain him and his family for the rest of their lives. So, the decrease in gains did not affect him that severely. Sarah and her family remained on as house servants, but they were paid for their services; and their wages surpassed anyone else in the same capacity.

Although Sarah and Nathaniel's decision to stay would not likely cause a stir, Peter knew that Marie and John's decision to remain there with their sons was a ticking time bomb. He racked his head daily trying to find a way to convince her to leave, but she would not budge. She would only reply that Thomas would never leave without her and she was not going to leave without him.

Marie was loyal to her husband because he had been good to her, but she also still loved John; and since she found out that John's mother was the daughter of a slave, her mind started entertaining thoughts of a life with him. She would find herself daydreaming of being able to raise their family together and love each other openly, but then she would push those thoughts out of her head. No matter what her feelings, Marie took her vows seriously; and in her mind, the only way she and Thomas would part would be in death.

Back in South Carolina, Jacob was still reeling from Thomas' death and how he was going to break the news   to his sister, but in order to do that he had to stay alive to deliver the message. As the war raged on, Jacob relied more and more on Lou. He became his life preserver and was the only thing that kept Jacob from drowning in guilt and grief. Lou constantly reminded him, that he owed it to Thomas to make it back to his family alive, so he had to stay.

With battle after battle, the 33rd continued to impress and surprise their commanders. The skill they showed in combat and the tenacity and drive to keep fighting ignited   a spirit they had never seen in their white counterparts; which Colonel. T. W. Higginson described in detail in his report to General Rufus Saxton. He raved about how the Black soldiers displayed an intuitive nature that gave them an advantage over their enemies; and that their commanding officers came to rely on that knowledge to develop their battle plans.

The raising of the first Black regiment provided slaves with the opportunity to fight for their freedom and display their skills as soldiers. It became clear that utilizing the Black soldiers was an asset that needed to be capitalized upon, so after the Emancipation Proclamation, the Union began to aggressively recruit more Black soldiers.

During that time America had an influx of Irish Catholic immigrants. Due to this population being generally poor, they vehemently opposed the emancipation of slaves; because they feared they would have to compete with freed Blacks for the scarce jobs available. In the beginning of the war, hundreds of them swarmed to volunteer, but after taking some heavy losses, the number of volunteers dramatically decreased.

In 1863, a large number of Irish Immigrants were signed up as citizens in a ploy to swell the machine vote. However, these immigrants didn't know that becoming a citizen also made them eligible for the draft. Angered over this realization, they responded by inciting what came to be known as the draft riot in New York City. Although there was a universal resistance to the draft, it was prominent   in Catholic areas. Rioters took to the street attacking buildings and destroying property in protest. Their efforts were thwarted by military forces.

One day while out on patrol, Thomas and Lou crossed paths with a White Union regiment. They were discussing what they were going to do when the war was over, when they happened upon a White Union soldier name Patrick Sweeney. Sweeney was of average height and stature, with pale white skin, fire red hair and eyes as green as a four leaf clover.

"Whatcha gon do when ya outta heh?" Lou asked, his English slowly improving from participating in the school the Military set up.

"I dunno yet. Guess I'll go back to North Carolina first an deliva da news 'bout Thomas to ma sista an parents; then I wus thanking 'bout goin on up to New Yawk an seein if deys sum wurk up dere. Nah dat we free, no tellin what I can do." Jacob said.

Laughing as he appeared out of the bushes, Patrick interrupted. "Oh ya darkies thinkin 'bout comin ta the big city now are ya? Well, ya jus wipe dat thought out yer heads right now. I don't need yer kine 'round takin food out me mouf. Barely 'nuff jobs now. So ya jus stay on down heh an peck sum cotton or sumthin." Patrick said, standing with his gun resting on his shoulder.

Jacob moved toward Patrick saying "Wat you got 'ganst us? We Union Solgas jus lak you."

Spitting on the ground Patrick retorted, "Ah ta hell wit da Union! I'm only in dis unifom 'cause I were tricked into it. Dey 'rounded a bunch of us up sayin we gon be citizens ifin we sine up ta vote. Dey didn't sey nuffin 'bout we'd al' so be puttin da draff! So yer cin save dat Union brotha hood sp'ech fer me. Ya ain't no brotha of mine; an iffin dey'll trick a white man, ya darkies bes kip ya eyes o'pn 'cause dey'll kill a nigger," Patrick said, and walked back to his group.

Lou and Jacob stood there for a moment looking at Patrick as he walked off, then Jacob said breathing heavy from the exchange. "Whas wrong wit dat man Lou? We free nah an we fightin, bleedin an dyin jes lak dem! Jes lak dem Lou! We good 'nuff ta die fo 'em, but not good 'nuff to wurk wit'em? If thangs gon be da same Lou, den wat is we fightin' fo?" Jacob asked. He looked at Lou, who had been silent the whole time.

Putting his hand on Jacob's shoulder, Lou answered, "Abaham Lecon kin set uh free; bet he can't mek 'dem 'cept us. Don't matta wat cola unifom we got; don't chan da cola of ah skin. Can't nuthin chan dat an dat ol Ishman only sayin wat da res of 'em thanking."

Jacob and Lou rejoined their regiment and tried to put their encounter with Patrick in the back of their minds, but Jacob never forgot it. He was more determined than ever that he was going to make something of himself and thought New York was the best place to start. He was not going to allow anyone to tell him that he was only good for taking bullets and picking cotton.

Patrick Sweeney didn't know it, but his encounter would serve as Jacob's inspiration to succeed in a world that was designed for his failure.

When they returned to camp, Jacob retrieved a book the teacher had given him to help him improve his reading ability. From that day forward, Jacob pushed himself to the limit in the field and in his studies. Day and night whenever he had the opportunity, Jacob practiced reading and speaking. He was determined to use whatever advantage and tools he could to improve his station and he began daydreaming about the day that he would return to North Carolina as a war hero and an educated man.

When Jacob learned to read and write well enough, he penned a letter home to his family, to tell them about his time in the military and about Thomas. It took him a long time to write the letter; not so much because of having difficulty spelling the words, but because he had difficulty finding the best way to tell his sister her husband wasn't coming home. Jacob had his teacher help him, by proofreading it and helping him correct his mistakes. He was adamant about perfecting his ability to use the English language. Even after his letter had been perfected, Jacob held onto it for months before he finally sealed the envelope and gave it to his sergeant to be mailed. He only wished his first letter had better news.

In North Carolina, things had pretty much taken on a rudimentary routine. The former slaves that remained on the Devereux plantation had adjusted to their new roles as sharecroppers; and Peter had adjusted to being a landlord. The thing he could not adjust to, was the fear that he woke up with each day that someone would find out about his family's secrets. It had been almost two years now and there had been no word from Thomas or Jacob and, yet their family still held onto hope. A hope that chained Marie to a promise to wait for her husband at all cost. Although Peter admired her loyalty, he hated that it could cost her and her family, his family, their life.

Just when it appeared Marie would be left to wait forever in limbo, loyal to a ghost and a life she would never again have, the letter arrived. The mailman rode up to the house to deliver the first and most heartbreaking letter they would ever receive. Sarah greeted him at the door and took the letter.

Since Sarah and Marie both came from Peter's plantation, they were both afforded an education and could read and write quite well. Sarah had begun teaching Nathaniel, until Peter hired a teacher to come in to provide formal instruction as he had on his previous plantation.

Marie was in the back room caring for the twins. Since Helena's departure, Marie was able to take on the role of mother for both of her sons. She hoped that Helena would stay gone forever and that with her absence, she would be free to love both boys openly. They had grown so much since Thomas had been away, and soon they would be celebrating their 8th birthday. Marie began thinking about celebrating her sons' birthday with Thomas and watching his eyes sparkle with pride when he saw how much they had grown while he was away. She was deep in thought when she heard her mother calling her in an excited tone

"Marie! Nate! Everybody come quickly!" Sarah called.

Peter and John came running from one end of the house and Marie and the boys came from the other. Nathaniel was outside tending to some yard work when he heard his wife calling him.

"Ya aight hummingbird?" Nathaniel asked as he burst through the door.

"What in the world happened, Sarah? You scared me half to death," Peter said, clutching his heart.

"Yeah mama, what's the matter?" Marie quizzed, holding the twin's hands. Sarah saw the frightened look on her family's faces and apologized.

"I'm sorry for scaring you all like that, but I was just excited. A letter came today from Jacob; and I thought everyone might want to hear about his and Thomas' adventures together," Sarah explained.

Once they realized the reason for the commotion, they all became just as excited to hear how their soldiers were doing. Peter gathered everyone in the parlor to take a seat and listen to Sarah read the letter. Once everyone was comfortably seated, Sarah opened the letter with a big smile on her face and began to read.

February 8, 1864

Dear Mama and Papa,

Today our regiment was renamed from the 1st South Carolina Infantry to the 33rd United States Colored Infantry. I guess since we have shown ourselves to be capable soldiers on the field of battle, they felt we deserved a new name. The Army set up schools here as well, so we could all learn to read and write; as you can see I have made the most it.

I found that I really like learning and plan to continue to explore all the wonderful opportunities the Army has to offer. I have had the honor of serving with some good men who have proved to be brave in battle, but none braver than Thomas. Since, we arrived here he looked out for me. He and another soldier we met here named Lou, have gotten me through some pretty rough times in battle; and had it not been for them, I don't know if I would have made it this far. Please tell Marie that Thomas kept his promise to stand with me until the end; which I am sorry to say came for Thomas much too soon.

As Sarah read that last line, the smile left her face; and in reading the next lines silently, she dropped the letter to the ground and tears began to stream down her face. The rest of the family, who had been attentively hanging on her every word, asked what was wrong as the feeling of dread filled the room.

"What does the rest of the letter say mama? Please mama, finish the rest of the letter. What happened to Thomas?" Marie asked frantically, but Sarah could not speak.

Marie picked up the fallen letter and continued to read. When she read what had caused her mother's reaction, Marie felt faint but forced herself to continue to read.

I know this letter has been a long time coming, but my lack of ability to write it and my lack of desire to break my sister's heart prevented its delivery. The night Thomas died; we were on a midnight march through the pines, when we were surrounded by confederate troops. Everyone in my company, including Thomas fired on the enemy and drove them into the woods. It was a hollow victory however, because when the smoke cleared, Thomas lay dead from a single bullet to the head.

The soldiers and I took his body back to camp and we buried him the next day. They had a small informal service for him and before he was committed to the ground, I took his insignias from his uniform to bring home to you in memoriam of his valiant service to his country. Mama, I know that Marie's heart is breaking right now, but tell her that he did not die in vain. I am going to continue his fight for freedom; and she must honor him by living her life. He would not want her to bury herself along with him.

Well, I have to close this letter now; we have to prepare for duty tomorrow. Please tell Papa and everyone else that I love and miss you all dearly. I will write again as soon as I can. Continue to pray for us all.

Love,
Jacob

Marie closed the letter and bent down to hold her son, who was lying on the ground sobbing uncontrollably. She didn't know what to do with herself. Thomas was her husband and she vowed to love and honor him until death they did part. She just didn't think death would part them so soon.
Everyone was silent as sadness crept over the room.

Peter informed everyone that he was going to prepare a small memorial for Thomas the next day, so everyone could say their goodbyes. Marie gave her appreciations for the gesture and went to her room to grieve in private. Peter went to his study to plan the small service and figure how to gently convince Marie that although she was grieving the loss of Thomas. She now had no reason to remain in a perilous situation.

Peter left to contact the old Quaker minister that he had spoken to before to see if he would still be able to help John, Marie and the twins to relocate to Canada. Once the minister confirmed he could still help, Peter told him to get things ready and he would bring them to him by the end of the week. On the way back home, Peter stopped in town and picked up a beautiful headstone for Thomas' memorial.

The next morning, everyone gathered in the garden for the service. The overcast clouds seemed to symbolize the sullen mood of everyone in attendance; but when the clouds remarkably disappeared leaving behind a beautiful clear sky, it was a comfort.

"He wit the angels now baby girl," Nathaniel said, as he comforted his daughter.

"I know Papa; I know," Marie said as she hugged him.

When the service was over, everyone retired to the house for refreshments; and Peter again presented his plan for John and Marie to leave.

"Marie, can I speak to you for a second?" Peter said, pulling Marie to the side. Peter didn't know how to begin the conversation without seeming insensitive, but he knew that time was of the essence. He had already spoken to Sarah and Nathaniel and they both now agreed with Peter that Marie and the boys should leave with John, but Peter was hoping he wouldn't have to bring them in to convince her.

"I want you to know that I am so sorry about Thomas and under any other circumstances I would not dare bring up anything to upset you on a day like today," Peter informed her as he searched for the words to say next.

Knowing what Peter was trying to say before he could say anything, Marie responded, "This is about me and the boys' leaving for Canada with John isn't it?"

Relieved that Marie had broached the subject for him, Peter answered, "Yes; but Marie…."

Interrupting him before he continued, Marie said, "When do we leave?"

Surprised, Peter stammered, "At the end of the week."

Without even looking at Peter, Marie replied with stoic expression. "We'll be ready." Then she returned to the parlor to rejoin her family in remembering her husband. She knew that with Thomas gone, she no longer had a reason to stay.

Chapter Eighteen

Home is Where the Heart is

Fall 1864

Marie prepared herself and her children for the trip to Canada. She knew that they would not be able to take a   lot with them, so she tried to choose what she would take very carefully. She searched about her tiny room looking   for things that she would take along: a necklace that her mother gave her; the blankets that she knitted for the boys when they were born; wooden toys that Thomas and her father made for them; a pocket knife that belonged to Jacob; and of course, the insignias from Thomas' Uniform that Jacob sent in his letter.

Marie packed her most precious belongings in a small bag along with a few items of clothing. Her mother packed some food and water in a bag for them to take along; and Peter packed a bag of money for them to start their new life and instructions on what to do once they reached Ohio and where to go when they reached Canada.

Although Canada did not abolish slavery until August 28, 1833 and it didn't become effective until August 1, 1834, the institution had already become severely strained by the 1820s. In fact, 1821 was the last year an advertisement for the sale of a slave appeared.

Canada had a long reputation for being a place where oppressed Blacks could seek refuge. Since 1815, thousands of slaves had escaped to Canada via the Underground Railroad and by 1852, conductors of the Underground Railroad were also using steamers to transport fugitive slaves.

The Black population was steadily growing in Canada and so many Blacks had migrated there, that on April 3, 1851, famous African American Abolitionist Frederick Douglass spoke to a crowd of 1200 people on the malevolence of American Slavery. Later that same year on September 10, 1851, the North American Convention of Colored Freeman was hosted in Toronto; and hundreds of Blacks came from England, Canada and the Northern United States to hear great speakers against slavery.

Peter filled Marie and her parents in on all that Canada had to offer and the more he talked about it, the more everyone began to agree that given the circumstances, Canada was the best choice for John and Marie to give themselves and their children a better life. Even though slavery had been abolished in the US, racism and extreme hatred had not; neither had some laws that would prevent John and Marie from being together.

In 1863 came the criminalization of interracial marriage, cohabitation, and in some cases sex known as miscegenation. Anti-miscegenation laws enforced that any form of intimate relationship between different races was illegal and punishable by law. For John and Marie, this meant that if anyone found out that they had children together they could be jailed. And even worse than the laws, were the lawless; if any of the thousands of rabid racists that populated the United States, found that John was Black and had been passing as a White man he could be killed.

The remainder of that week Marie, John and the boys spent most of their time with Sarah, Nathaniel and Peter and tried to soak up as many memories as they could. They had their final dinner as a family on Thursday and went to meet the Minister on Friday to leave.

When they arrived at the minister's house, they were told where they were supposed to hide until it was time to meet the boat later that night. The boys were restless, and Marie and John tried to make them as comfortable as they could.

"Mama, are we ever going to see grandma and grandpa again?" TJ asked, looking sad.

"Of course, we will baby. We are just going on a little adventure; and we will come back to visit soon, okay?" Marie said.

"Okay," TJ said slowly, still looking sad.

Then John Jr. asked, "Why isn't my mommy going with us? Where is she?" Marie had not prepared to have to face these questions yet, so she was searching for answers.

She knew that now was not the time to tell them the truth about she and John being their real parents, but she didn't know how to respond either.

"So many questions for such little boys, let's just try to get some rest and we will talk about all of this later," Marie said, trying to maintain her composure, but looking at the sweet innocent faces of her sons made it difficult.

John saw that Marie was becoming stressed and he tried to distract the boys from asking her any more questions. He entertained the boys with stories about the magical adventure on which they were about to embark.

"Get some rest boys, because in just a little while we will be leaving to start our adventure!" John said.

"Tell us about the adventure daddy!" John Jr exclaimed with excitement.

"Yes Mr. Devereux, tell us!" TJ echoed.

"Okay, I will tell you, but you have to lie down and get under the covers first; and you have to promise to go right to sleep after," John said, tickling the boys.

"We promise!" the boys said in unison and lay down under the covers as instructed. Once they were snug in the bed, John began telling them about going traveling on the magical path called the Underground Railroad to the Lake of Freedom. Then, taking the small row boat across this lake, where they were going to board a large ship. He told them that they would meet other boys and girls and families on the boat like them; and they were all going to live in a new land where anything was possible. Soon, the excited little boys drifted off to sleep; and Marie began to remember why she fell in love with John in the first place. He had a talent for making anything seem magical.

Around midnight, the old minister who was their conductor, woke them to leave. John reminded the boys of the importance of being quiet while they made their way to the next station on the Underground Railroad. They stopped, and the old minister gave the secret knock to let the station masters know they had arrived. John and his family were given food and fresh water, and led down to a hidden basement where other families were also hiding. When night came again they and the other families followed their conductor to their next stop.

After three long weeks of hiding and running to the next station, picking up additional people along the way, they finally reached Oberlin, Ohio. Standing in a state free of slavery, Marie smelled the sweet air of freedom for the first time.

"Mama, why you smiling and crying at the same time? You, all right?" TJ asked, looking up at Marie.

Wrapping her arms around her son, Marie replied, "I'm more than all right son; I'm free!"

The conductor led his passengers to a low white house called the Bardwell House, which was their final stop in the United States. The passengers were informed that they would be remaining at this station for a little while, because they had to wait for the steamer to arrive that would take them on to their final destination of Canada. When they were directed to the tiny attic where they would be sleeping, Marie and the boys were so exhausted from their travels, that they slept well into the next afternoon. John however, was up early talking to their gracious hostess.

The old woman had made a hot breakfast of bacon, eggs and toast, as well as a fresh pot of coffee. She joined John at the table, sitting his breakfast down in front of him.

Overwhelmed by her selfless act of helping them, John said, "Thank you so much for allowing me and my family to stay with you."

The comment caught the old woman off guard, but she had suspected by John's demeanor that he was connected to the beautiful young Black woman and to the two children, who were only distinguished by their complexion.

"It's my pleasure, young man. You know in Oberlin, there are vast numbers of free Blacks, so you don't have to hide in the daytime. No one would be suspicious of your being here; and the Blacks and Whites here attend school and even worship together. Once your family wakes from their rest, you should walk around town. It will likely be the first time you've been able to do so freely I suspect," the old woman said. She was smiling as she took away John's empty coffee cup and saucer.

"Yes ma'am; it will be," John replied with a smile, and then went to check on Marie and the boys.

When he entered the tiny attic, his family was just waking up. Marie yawned and stretched, trying to get her bearings.

"Good morning," John said with a smile.

Smiling back, Marie replied, "Good morning to you too; what smells so good downstairs?"

Laughing at how cute Marie looked with her hair all disheveled, John replied, "Our hostess, made breakfast and a fresh pot of coffee." Marie's eyes opened wide and a smile formed on her lips at the thought of a delicious breakfast. She woke the kids, so they could join her downstairs. John told them what the old woman said about the people of Oberlin and they all agreed to walk around the town to explore after breakfast.

As John and Marie took their sons on a tour of the town, they were all amazed at what they saw. Black and White people working together building structures; children of all races attending school together and learning to read and write; and people genuinely getting along. It was like they were in a dream and Marie could see herself settling down right here, but the reality was that even though Oberlin was not like North Carolina, they still would not be able to enjoy the same freedoms they could in Canada. They finished their tour around town and went back to the Bardwell House to rest up for the last leg of their journey. Tomorrow they would be Canadians.

Marie and John made sure they had all of their belongings, and after eating and resting for a while, the conductor led them to the waiting row boat at the edge of the lake. Marie walked quietly behind the Minister with her head covered and holding TJ's hand; John followed behind them holding John Jr.

The woods were so dark you could hardly see your hand before your face and each person held on to the person ahead of them to ensure no one got lost. Even though slavery had been abolished the previous year, the war still raged on and the danger was still very real.

When they reached the small row boat, John and the Minister helped Marie and the children aboard, before looking around to see if anyone was watching. Once they were confident they were alone, John boarded as well; and helped the Minister row out to the waiting steamer. John's heart was thumping hard in his chest. He felt like it was in sync with his rowing; and it increased the closer he got to the steamer. He tried to stay focused on the ship, but his mind was racing with thoughts of what would happen if they were caught.

Looking at Marie's face, he could see she mirrored his anxiety; and he quickly tried to hide his fears in order to calm hers. Like it or not, John was the head of this family and it was his job to take care of Marie and his sons; and that meant making them feel that everything was going to be alright, even if he wasn't sure they would be himself.

After what seemed like an eternity, they finally reached the ship. The Minister gave the signal to the captain and he allowed them to board. Since they were the last people they were expecting, the Captain immediately got underway once they were safely aboard. The minister then waved goodbye and rowed back to shore. This was as far as he went. His job was done and now those on board the ship would take over.

"Come this way and I will show you were you can put your belongings and get some food." A small framed white woman said as she led them down a narrow corridor to a room with a multitude of cots and blankets. John and his family followed the woman over to a space where they could settle in for the long journey.

While Marie and her children were escaping to freedom, Jacob was still fighting for it. It was now 1865 and the battles appeared to be coming to an end. On April 9, 1865, Confederate General Robert E. Lee surrendered at Appomattox Courthouse in Virginia; six days later, President Lincoln was shot by a southern sympathizer named John Wilkes Booth.

After Lee surrendered, Confederate Generals across the south followed suit. President Andrew Johnson (who took over after Lincoln was shot) officially declared an end to the war one month later on May 9, 1865. Lincoln's influence prompted Congress to sanction the 13th amendment on December 6, 1865; freeing the 65,000 slaves that remained in the United States and making slavery officially illegal.

During the times of war, it was not just the Blacks that feared being caught by the Confederates. Captured Union soldiers of both races were being placed in the most inhumane prison camps. The most notorious camp, Andersonville, was a prison in Georgia where Union soldiers were kept in deplorable conditions until most of them died.

Disease and starvation claimed the lives of almost 13,000 Union soldiers confined in Andersonville before the war ended and the prisoners were released. One White Union soldier was literally reduced to a veil of skin covering bones when he was liberated from Andersonville. Henry Wirz was the Prison's Commandment. After the war was over, he stood trial for the atrocities committed at Andersonville and was executed.

Although the war was over, Jacob remained with Company A until January 31, 1866 when it was disassembled. He and the other members of his company received Medals of Honor for their service; and he fulfilled his promise that he would return home a war hero. Now that he had accomplished that goal, Jacob vowed to complete his other goal as well; to amass as much success and wealth as he could. Maybe he would one day go to Canada and try to find his sister. Whatever he decided to do with his life, Jacob was determined that from this point on, it would be just that; his life. After a brief stop in North Carolina to see his parents, Jacob had planned head to New York to start building that new life.

In Canada, John and Marie had gotten settled in. It was so different from the United States that it almost seemed like a different world, but each still longed for their family back in the states. They purchased a small house and Marie worked to take care of it and their children; although she was quite taken with writing. She was interested to learn about an African American novelist named Harriet E. Wilson, who wrote her autobiography entitled

Sketches from the Life of a Free Black, in 1859. This inspired Marie to possibly pen her own novel someday.

The children were enrolled in school; and John began working for a local politician and found that he had an undiscovered love for it. He was still passing as white and was becoming quite the favorite in his office. He felt some guilt over his deception, but he still wasn't comfortable revealing his secret to the world.

TJ and John Jr were adjusting well to their new environment, but they still did not know that Marie and John were their parents. This was another secret that ate away at John's soul, but he couldn't find a way to convey the story to his sons. How do you tell your children that something as important as their origin and their identity, the very thing they thought was absolute and unchanging, was all a lie? How could he tell John Jr that his mother is not a wealthy White socialite, but the former slave that served her? How could he tell TJ that his father was not an honored Black war hero who died in battle, but the man his mother worked for?

John and Marie both knew that there could be consequences whether they told the truth or continued the lie; the question was which would have the least possible damage. Their sons were growing up with false identities and John's burgeoning political career was built on a foundation of false pretenses. Although they moved to a new place and had a new life, they still harbored old secrets; and as they both knew from past experience, secrets never stay buried for long.

The Saga Continues…

Secrets on Tobacco Road is the first in a series of books that will chronicle the lives, loves and lies that intertwine the Devereux, Marchand, and Jean Baptiste families. Whatever became of Helena Marchand Devereux? Did Jacob fulfill his goal of becoming successful? Will TJ and John Jr find out who their parents really are? Will John's secrets come back to haunt his political career? The answer to these questions and much more will be revealed in the forthcoming, second installment entitled My Secrets to Keep. Until then, keep watching; you never know what's going to happen next!

www.ingramcontent.com/pod-product-compliance
Lightning Source LLC
Chambersburg PA
CBHW070745180626
46818CB00007B/2995